BACK TO BUNKER HILL

LOVE THROUGHOUT TIME

BOOK THREE

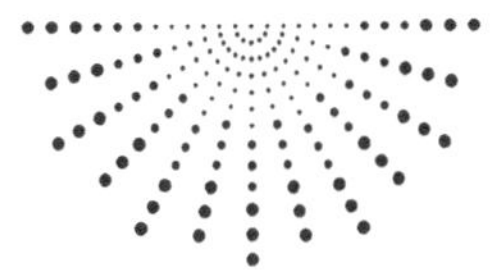

ID JOHNSON

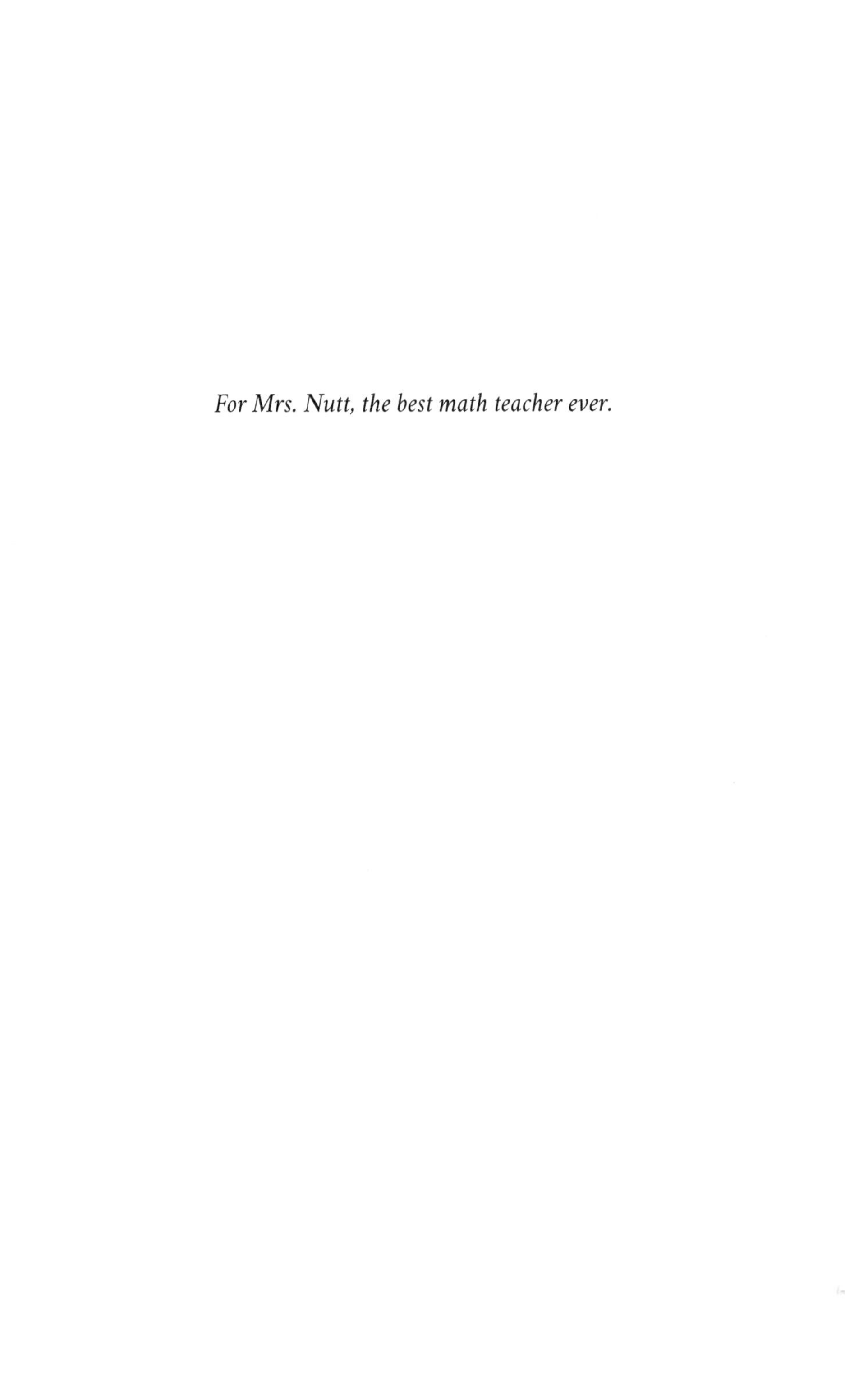

For Mrs. Nutt, the best math teacher ever.

CONTENTS

CHAPTER ONE

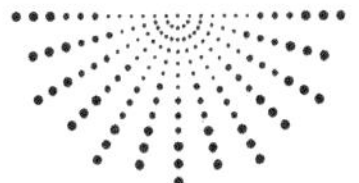

"Your great uncle wanted you to understand how important our family was in the creation of this country."

The tone in my Great Aunt Ida's voice matches the vibe of this house, a large, imposing building that has stood well over two hundred fifty years—quiet yet confident, assured that her place as a member of our family, along with all the years she and her husband, Great Uncle Arthur, had dedicated to the community is solid.

I instantly wish I could have gotten to know her more and that I'd had more time with Uncle Arthur before he passed away. My sister and I knew them, of course, but mainly as distant relatives who showed up for weddings and family reunions. I've been told about this house but never laid eyes on it until yesterday.

Aunt Ida sits gracefully in the ornate, American rococo chair across from us and crosses her ankles, her black tailored dress and flawless grey updo suited to her proud status as a member of the Monroe family, descendants of one of the original colonial families in America. Though I'm a Miller, she's always told me we're all true

Monroes, including my dad, since Aunt Ida is also a Monroe by marriage.

She wears a soft smile on her face despite just losing her husband of fifty-five years. Only a slight slump in her shoulders reveals how tired she must be even after hundreds of well-wishers have left the house after the funeral reception. It's a relief he's not suffering anymore after such a long illness. Still, to lose the love of a lifetime…. I can't even imagine how that must feel.

I hope someday to find someone I can fall in love with as deeply as the two of them were. Looking at the photos of them that sit behind Aunt Ida on a bureau, it's quite clear how in love they were. From their wedding photo to a picture taken last Christmas, they're gazing at one another in such a way that makes my heart sing for them.

Someday, I hope to find someone who looks at me the way Uncle Arthur looks at her, someone I can spend the rest of my life with.

My mom enters the room and puts a hand on Aunt Ida's shoulder. Since my grandparents died a few years ago, she's been thinking of Aunt Ida and Uncle Arthur as the closest thing she has to parents. Uncle Arthur was my grandpa's brother. She's been visiting often during his illness. Guilt rushes over me since I was too busy with the end of the school year to come with her, though everyone insisted I tend to my students first.

Mom, along with the rest of us, has been doing what she can to comfort Aunt Ida since Uncle Arthur's passing. Naturally, the service was upsetting, but since we got back to the house for the reception, Aunt Ida's been in better spirits. Now, she's asked all of us in the younger generation to join her here in the parlor.

"Maybe you should rest," Mom suggests. "It's been a long day."

Aunt Ida shakes her head and pats Mom's hand as it rests on her shoulder. "I'm just fine. Your uncle led a long, full life, and we should celebrate it. I want all of the younger members of the family to understand their heritage, as he would have wanted."

Mom nods, letting out a light sigh. Yesterday was the first time I've seen her in two weeks. Nina, Dad, and I flew in for the service. I was surprised to see how tired Mom looked. In contrast to Aunt Ida, she has dark circles under eyes, indicating she could use some rest herself. "Can I at least get you some herbal tea?"

"That would be lovely, thank you," Aunt Ida tells her before turning back to us. "I'd like to share some history with you." Her blue eyes, slightly red from crying, admire each of us one at a time, first my three cousins, Joe, Tom, and Harry, then my sister Nina, alighting on me last. "It's such a joy to see you all together."

I've always been a curious soul, so my ears perk up at her mysterious statement. "What sort of history would you like to share with us, Aunt Ida?"

"Well, my Arthur was very interested in the Revolutionary War, particularly the Battle of Bunker Hill," she begins. "Did you know that happened only eight miles away?"

I nod, but I doubt anyone else in the room has much knowledge on the subject. All of them are teenagers. Who needs to study American history when you can watch videos on TikTok? Still, they're polite enough to nod along as Aunt Ida begins to tell her story.

"The Monroes who lived in this house at the time sent their children to fight for our country's freedom," she explains. "Sadly, one of them did not come home."

"That's awful," Nina whispers, and everyone solemnly agrees.

My eyes flutter around the room, taking in all the antique furniture and decor. The light scent of honey lingers in the air from the beeswax candles lit on the wide stone fireplace. This parlor, along with the rest of the home, appears frozen in time, the furnishings all in ornately carved cherry wood with soft, floral fabrics that date back to colonial times. Of course, there have clearly been quite a few updates to modernize the home, especially with the appliances, bathroom fixtures, and air conditioning. But the heart of the home is clearly the way it stood so many years ago.

I've been eager to explore every inch of the place, especially after strolling by the immense library when we arrived yesterday, but all the preparations, the funeral, and reception today have made that impossible… so far.

"The family kept extensive records of the activities near here," Aunt Ida continues.

With a sharp inhale, I turn back to Aunt Ida, wondering what incredible historical documents might be found in that breathtaking library down the hall, its solid wood shelves full all the way to the ceiling. Did she say one of the Monroe children didn't make it?

"At the time, Boston was under siege," she continues. "The citizens had learned that the British intended to occupy all the surrounding hills, which would give them full control of the city and the harbor. This would allow them to land enough ships for unlimited soldiers to occupy the colonies. If that had been achieved, there would likely have never been a United States of America."

I notice my sister and cousins leaning forward a bit, listening intently.

Mom returns, setting a teacup beside Aunt Ida. She thanks her, lifts it, and takes a sip before continuing. "Your uncle collected a series of letters from soldiers describing the battles on the Charlestown peninsula. Many of them spent time in this house after the battle as it served as a hospital for a spell."

As she takes another sip, the magnificent mahogany grandfather clock in the corner strikes the hour. Chills rush over me as I realize that those soldiers probably looked at the very same clock, admiring its gold leaf detail on the finely carved wood.

Aunt Ida continues her history lesson. "The same can be said for the house next door. The Thomas family owns the adjoining property. They had quite a role in the war themselves. They also own the cottage."

"What cottage?" Nina asks.

"Oh, have I never mentioned it to you?" We all shake our heads, enraptured by her mysterious tale. "It sits right off the edge of our property to the south, dear," Aunt Ida explains. "It's tucked away in a wooded area. You could walk right past it and not see it if you didn't know it was there."

I get a strange flutter in my heart I can't explain. What is it about this cottage that's so important?

"Who lives there?" Harry asks.

"Nobody," Aunt Ida replies. "Oh, it's a lovely little cottage, hand-built by a young man just before the Revolutionary War. It's a sturdy sandstone house with fine woodwork, some of which is more impressive than the wood in this home, which was all handmade. The young man was a fine craftsman. He took his time perfecting every detail." She looks up just long enough to nod toward Mom, who refills her teacup. "But it's haunted of course," she adds nonchalantly, as if she hasn't been leading up to this moment all along.

Aunt Ida has always been quite the storyteller.

Nina tilts her head to the side, her eyes so wide she reminds me of my students when we covered Poe. My baby sister definitely doesn't share my love of all things paranormal. "Haunted?" I try not to giggle at the tremble in her voice.

"Yes, of course," Aunt Ida continues. "Often the ghosts that roam this property can be seen heading toward the cottage."

"Ghosts? Plural?" Nina clarifies, and Aunt Ida nods and laughs.

"That is so cool," Joe, my youngest cousin, says, awestruck.

I restrain a chuckle, remembering why we're here in the first place, but I can't say I disagree with him.

"It is quite 'cool,'" Aunt Ida replies, lingering on the word.

"Have you seen one?" Harry asks.

She takes a slow sip of her tea and says nothing for a moment, but when she sets down the cup, the side of her lip curls up as she adjusts her shawl.

Nina shakes her head. "Well, I can tell you right now, if I see a freaking ghost, I'm getting out of here! You won't be able to catch me!"

"Nina," Mom says, shaking her head at my sister's ridiculousness.

But Aunt Ida waves her off and leans toward Nina. "It's quite all right, dear. You don't have to worry. All the ghosts here are friendly, and they know not to show themselves to those who might be frightened. Now, the same can't be said for the ghosts at the cottage. If you pay the cottage a visit, well, there's no telling what you may see."

I sit in silence while the boys ask more questions about the ghosts that Aunt Ida's seen in her home, but I'd like to hear more about the buildings on the property, especially the cottage. Somehow, I can already picture it in my mind.

"Can we please stop talking about ghosts now?" Nina asks after a few minutes.

I have to laugh this time, and I'm grateful for the opening to change the subject. "What was the name of the man who lived in the cottage?"

Aunt Ida shakes her head nearly imperceptibly. "No one ever lived there. Sadly, he died in the war before he could move in. Such a beautiful little home never occupied in all these years."

I tilt my head in confusion. "After all this time, why not?"

"Well, the family would never allow anyone to live in it or tear it down, and they certainly wouldn't sell it," she explained. "The Thomases always insisted he was coming back." She looks around at us all. "It's true. Generation after generation of the Thomases are said to believe that Eric Thomas is coming back. Isn't that unusual?"

A shiver runs down my spine. But it's not one of fear like I'm guessing my sister is experiencing right now. No, this is a warm bolt of electricity, a sensation I haven't felt before that wraps around me and envelops my whole body. Eric Thomas—why does... whatever this feeling is... stir in me at the sound of his name? And why would his whole family think he's coming back after being killed in the war? Maybe they had reason to believe he survived the war. Still, the war was two hundred fifty years ago. He couldn't possibly come back now—unless he's one of the ghosts out there.

Aunt Ida moves on to a story about another family, but it's hard to pay attention as Eric's name haunts my mind. I wonder whether my aunt has seen his ghost, or if she knows more about the story than she's letting on. I don't want to bring it up now since the others are asking questions about the other family now, the one that lives on the other side of Aunt Ida's property.

My heart quickens as I imagine seeing the haunted cottage for myself. I picture a small structure with an inviting porch, wide windows, and finely crafted woodwork around the porch. Inside, I imagine a cozy fireplace, a bedroom or two, and a kitchen with a warm hearth and handcrafted cabinets.

As Aunt Ida begins to talk about our own family that lived here during the time of the Revolutionary War, I try to concentrate, but it's difficult. There's clearly more to this place than I've ever realized. In the next week, while I stay to help Aunt Ida around the house, I hope to get a chance to explore every inch of the property–and one other place….

Unable to concentrate on her next story, I make up my mind. Tonight, I'm going to visit that cottage and see for myself if the spirit of Eric Thomas still lingers there. Hopefully, I can talk my sister and cousins into going with me. If not, well, I'll just have to do it on my own.

I don't think I can sleep until I see that place for myself.

CHAPTER TWO

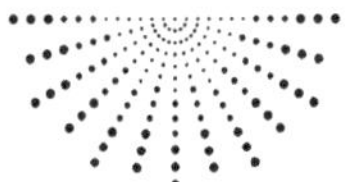

HATTIE

THE LIGHT OF THE RISING MOON, A FEW STARS, AND A COUPLE OF OLD flashlights we found in the garage light the way as we take the path Aunt Ida mentioned leads to the old cottage. It's early evening, not quite dark, but we wanted to be prepared. I take my time, even though I'm excited to see the place, not wanting to trip and hurt myself. I've been known to be a bit klutzy, after all, and this is no time for a twisted ankle.

"Are you sure it's even legal for us to be wandering around out here?" Nina hangs behind me, clearly still frightened.

I shake my head at her for about the tenth time. "We're still on Monroe property. There's nothing stopping us from exploring."

"Except a forest," she complains, stopping and putting her hands on her hips. "Aunt Ida made it sound like it was just on the edge of the property–like in a few trees and bushes. If it's over there, that's an understatement."

"It's actually nice and shady out here," I argue, lifting my gaze to the thick canopy above. The bushy hemlocks meet above us in a tent of green. Below, their trunks are so thick, they must be older than the Monroe estate itself.

"Stop being annoying, Nina," Joe snaps. "I want to see this cottage."

"Yeah," Tom agrees. "You were up for it before we left."

"I was up for it before I knew we'd be traipsing through a forest," Nina retorts. "How do we even know we aren't lost?"

"I'm sure the cottage is up ahead," I tell her. "Aunt Ida said it was to the south, and that's the way we're going. We're on the path she said to take."

Finally, Nina starts walking again, though she lags behind, the boys all several feet in front of us, making better time.

"Oh. There it is," Harry says after a moment.

I hitch a breath as we step into a clearing, at the center of which is a small stone cottage. I bite down on my lower lip, my heart thumping hard in my chest. Slowly, I approach the building, but the boys take off. Well, if there were any ghosts here, they've got to be scared away now.

When I get closer, it's obvious Aunt Ida was right. The Thomas family has taken great care of the place, keeping the small yard in front of it mowed and the bushes surrounding it trimmed, turning the place into an oasis of sorts in the middle of the forest.

The image I conjured in my mind earlier isn't far off. The cottage is such a perfect, adorable little home, made of sandstone with beautiful carved oak trim around the windows and doors. The roof looks relatively new, but that makes sense as it has probably been replaced if the house is really two hundred and fifty years old. The quaint front porch is also made of stone, warm and inviting with a carved wood railing supporting rectangular planter boxes full of recently tended flowers. It's as if the whole place is just waiting for its owner to return.

Eric Thomas—they say he'll come back one day.

I step up on the stone porch, inhaling the minty scent of wild bergamot growing in the planter boxes. The Thomas family clearly took their job of preserving the place seriously. Do they really believe

Eric will return after all this time? It seems so far-fetched, yet they've gone to such trouble to preserve this place.

"This is so cool," Joe says, smooshing his face up against the glass of a window. "Can we go inside?"

A twinge of excited energy flows through me. I want to go in, too —I feel like, for some reason, I should go inside, but the fact that I'm standing on this porch means we aren't on Aunt Ida's property anymore.

I open my mouth to say that, but Harry is already trying the door. "It's locked." He shakes his head. "Should we break in?"

"Definitely not," I tell him, though a strange ache in my heart seems to be pulling me toward the entryway. Instead, I press my hand against the sandstone wall. It's gritty, like sandpaper, but also warm, maybe from absorbing the heat of the sun all day, though even in this clearing, the trees shade the house well. It seems strange that it seems so inviting under the circumstances.

"Don't you dare break in," Nina scolds him. "Remember, this is on the Thomas's property, not Aunt Ida's."

"Yeah, you're right," Harry agrees. "But the outside is so cool," he adds, patting the front of the house with his hand. "I wanna see the inside. That guy who built it must have spent a lot of time and effort on it. Look at the incredible detail in this carved wood."

I follow his gaze to see that close up, every inch of the exterior is tightly constructed. "It's amazing."

"Eric was his name, right?" Nina asks.

"Right. Eric Thomas." Those strange, pleasant tingles return as I say his name.

Nina walks up closer and puts her hand on a window. "Why does the glass look like this?"

"It's because it's old," I explain. "Glass seems solid, but it's actually viscous and flows, but not enough that we can even tell in our lifetimes. But with something this old, you can notice that it's been pulled by gravity to the bottom." I step over to another window. "See? This one has been replaced. It must have broken or something and the Thomas family fixed it. Usually, only wealthy people could afford glass back then." I suppose Eric Thomas wanted only the best for his cottage and did what needed to be done to secure the glass for his windows.

"Hmm." Nina's eyes shift back and forth between the two windows, comparing the glass. "I guess all those books you read pay off eventually."

I let out a giggle. "I guess so."

"I'm sure the Thomases won't mind if we look around," Tom says impatiently. "I want to see the back."

"I'm going with you." Harry steps off the porch to follow him, and Joe is not far behind them.

"Be careful," I call out, but the boys have already disappeared around the corner.

Nina's lips disappear into a thin line, and she shakes her head. "I'll go make sure they don't do something stupid."

"Okay. I'd like to look around here for a bit first."

"Be right back," she says before taking the flashlight from my hand and following the boys, shining the light in the direction where they disappeared.

I run my hands over the wooden railing, feeling its smooth finish. It must have been replaced at some point since the solid oak would have weathered out here, but given how much attention to detail has been taken with the cottage's upkeep, I'm guessing it looks similar to the railing it replaced. Stepping down off the porch, I take a seat on the step and admire the view of the yard and forest surrounding it. I look up at the trees for a moment, then close my eyes, listening to the sounds of night creatures coming from every direction. It's so peaceful here. It somehow feels like home.

Opening my eyes, my body jerks to attention as I think I catch sight of movement out of the corner of my eye. Turning my head, I see the outline of a familiar shape off in the trees. At first, I think it looks like the shape of a man–but that's impossible. Squinting, I lean forward, and the shape takes further form–a tall man with dark hair, walking between the trees.

A shiver goes down my spine. I blink a few times, thinking he'll disappear, but I can still see him.

"H-Hello?"

He doesn't answer, so I get up, my heart racing as I run over to the trees he walked past… but he's gone. I take a few more steps into the forest, but I don't see him anywhere. He's just disappeared.

"What the hell?" I whisper out loud. "Was that a man—or a ghost?" My hand over my heart, I try to catch my breath. While part of me is a bit scared, the rest is flabbergasted, and thrilled. That feeling I got earlier, when Aunt Ida was talking about the cabin, floods over me. What if that was him?

"Who are you talking to?"

I yelp and spin around, my heart up in my throat as the flashlight reveals my sister's curious face. "Shit, Nina!" I scold her. "Don't scare me like that!"

"See? It's creepy out here." She laughs wickedly, and I have to wonder if she didn't do that on purpose.

"It's not creepy when no one is sneaking up on you." I fold my arms under my chest. "It's beautiful. Where are the boys?"

"Still out back. You'd better come see this. They won't listen to me."

"See what?" But she's already walking and ignores me, so I follow her around to the back of the cottage where the boys are leaning over something, staring down at a circular hole in the ground, covered by a grate that looks like it's ready to cave in.

"Don't fall in," Joe warns as I approach.

"Um, yeah," I agree, seeing the ripples of water down below. "That's an old well. The last thing we need is for one of you to slip."

"Why not?" Tom asks. "We've got a lifeguard right here."

"I used to be a lifeguard," I correct him. "While I do coach the swim team, my skills relate to swimming pools, not deep, old wells with smooth sides and no way out without a rope or a ladder, which we don't have. Now, back away from it before you fall in."

"We'd better get back anyway," Nina says. "I'm gonna need a shower before dinner thanks to this trek through the forest."

I look back up at the little house, and my heart flutters again. I don't want to leave this place. I also can't stop thinking about the man I saw in the forest—at least, I think I saw someone. It's only seven o'clock. Maybe he'd be more willing to show himself nearer the witching hour. The whole place has a vibe I'd like to explore later at night anyway.

Maybe I'll wait until everyone else is asleep and come back here then.

Nina and I are both freshly showered when it's finally time for a late dinner. Aunt Ida sits at the head of the table wearing a light blue outfit that looks like she's ready to attend a dinner party. She's always been well dressed, though I've only really seen her at formal occasions when everyone else was, too. Still, I'm glad to see her out of the black suit and wearing something more cheerful.

Nina and I bring out the last of the side dishes and sit next to each other. The table is full of a colorful mix of vegetables, meats, and other side dishes, with the incredible scents of cheese and garlic filling the air from Mom's signature pasta dish. It's enough food for an army, but with the four teenage boys at the table with us, there won't be many leftovers.

"Mom, sit down," I insist. The dark circles under her eyes are even more pronounced than they were earlier. "I'm sure Sally can handle the rest." Mom insisted on helping with dinner, though Aunt Ida has a maid to help her take care of the huge estate. Sally is also an amazing cook. I know staying busy keeps Mom from thinking about Uncle Arthur, but she needs to rest, too. Thankfully, she sits and joins the rest of us.

Halfway through my salad, I lean toward Nina. "Let's go back to the cottage later tonight," I whisper.

"What?" she whisper/yells. "I don't think so."

"Please? I want to see what it's like out there in the dark, but I don't think I should take the boys since they're so rambunctious."

"No way," she says—a bit louder than a whisper, shaking her head.

She shoves a bite of pasta in her mouth, marking the conversation as over.

A few heads turn toward us, but I just smile. "This is really good."

"It is quite delicious," Aunt Ida agrees. "Sally is a wonderful cook, and Mary, your pasta is also tasty. Thank you."

Mom smiles, though it doesn't reach her tired eyes, and I'm glad to see her almost finished with her food.

After dinner, I pull Nina aside in the hallway behind the kitchen. "You've got to go out there with me," I insist. "Nothing will happen to us since we'll be together."

"Why do you want to go out there this time of night?" she asks.

I lift my shoulders in a shrug. "I don't know. It was so intriguing earlier. I didn't really get a chance to look around. I just think it'll be… neater this late at night." I can hardly tell her I want to see if that ghost appears again–if that's even what I truly saw.

"I can think of a thousand reasons to stay away," she insists. "We could fall and hurt ourselves. You know what a klutz you can be. And I'm not carrying you out of a forest with a broken leg, that's for sure."

"I'm not going to fall." I shake my head. "We'll each have a flash-light this time. Please, Nina? Just this once?"

She folds her arms over her chest. "No way. I went with you earlier, and I don't need to go again. We'll get lost!"

"We won't get lost," I argue.

"Well, we could," she insists. "It's too dangerous, and there's no way I'm going out there this late at night. You'd better not do it either since you'll be on your own!"

"Nina…."

"No means no!" She spins around and walks off, and I'm left in the hallway behind the kitchen watching her strut away.

I let out a gentle sigh and shake my head. I used to be able to convince Nina to do anything, but now that we don't live in the same house anymore, my sway over her has lessened.

Looking around, I realize even this part of the house is interesting. Back here in the area that must have been a servant's quarters when it was first built, there is stunning attention to detail. The doorway consists of a mahogany archway with intricately carved details, beveled on every inch with a floral carved keystone.

Seeing all of this attention to detail makes my heart ache to see more of the cottage, which was even stunning from the outside. I know I won't be able to go inside, but I feel the need to return, to admire it all in the moonlight, though even I can't explain why.

Like a siren's call, Eric Thomas's home calls to me.

Or is it Eric Thomas himself?

A shudder goes down my spine, and my mind's made up. I'm going back out there tonight for certain, whether Nina comes with me or not.

CHAPTER THREE

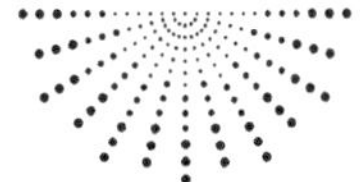

HATTIE

"NINA!" I'M ALMOST PANTING WHEN I FINALLY REACH THE HALLWAY where my sister disappeared a few moments ago.

She turns, having only made it halfway down the hall. "I said I'm not going."

I raise my hands as I approach her. "I know. I'm not asking you to. But don't you want to explore the estate with me? I'm sure we won't see any ghosts with so many people around."

Her lips contort into a half frown as she looks up at the ceiling, then back at me. "Okay, but we'd better not."

That took a lot of convincing. I shake my head as she follows me out of the room. "Let's start down here."

We pass under a large mahogany archway at the end of the hall. "This looks cozy," she says. "It must be the living room."

"I think it would have been called the drawing room back then, but you're right."

"Do you think all the furniture in the whole house is antique?" She runs her fingers along the velvety sofa cushions.

"Probably, especially that sofa." Stepping forward to admire it, I stop short as I catch sight of a portrait above the fireplace. A man and woman stand together, their blue eyes gazing warmly into the room.

"I guess those are the Monroes who used to live here."

Nina's voice gives me a start; I hadn't realized she was standing so close to me. Now, who's afraid? The couple look so in love, and I can see traces of my family members in their expressions. I can't take my eyes off the portrait. "Yes, they must be."

"I'd love wearing dresses like that all the time."

I left my eyebrows in surprise. The dress looks awfully uncomfortable to me, especially knowing there are so many layers underneath. I do admire the ruffled sleeves and paisley pattern. "My students would think I'd lost my mind if I came to school in something like that. But yes, it's pretty. This is probably a wedding portrait. They still look young."

She nods, and we move on. "Let's go look at the office," she suggests. "I saw a desk in there that looks interesting."

I'm anxious to see the rest of the house, but I can't resist another glance back at the portrait before exiting the room. While it's clear they are very much in love, I think I see a hint of something else in their eyes, especially the woman. I wonder when this was painted, how close to the Revolution the portrait was made. Is that fear hidden there so skillfully by the artist's brush? Excitement? Uncertainty? I'm not sure. It would be interesting to know how they felt about living in such a tumultuous time. Did they know the impact their generation would have on the rest of the world or were they completely unaware?

Sadly, I'll never know.

After fully exploring the rest of the first floor, we finally reach the library, a room I've wanted to visit since arrival. The moment I open the door to the vast archive, I'm speechless. Sturdy mahogany bookshelves reach all the way to the ceiling. The scent of leather and wood permeates the air, along with a hint of some sort of air freshener. I'm surprised it's not musty at all in here given the age of some of these books, though it is cooler in here and dimly lit, with reading lights on a couple of desks far away from most of the collection.

I'm frozen in the doorway for a moment, overwhelmed by the impressive collection. I can't imagine just how much knowledge and history are captured in all the pages of this library,

"Well, this looks like a place you'll be in for hours." Nina sighs and backs away. "I'm gonna go grab a snack and stream a movie in our room."

"Okay." It barely registers that she's leaving the room. My eyes flicker from one leather bound tome to the next, my fingers practically itching to dig into them.

She giggles and pats my shoulder. "Have fun!"

It's impossible to choose one thing to read. Some books bound with intricately decorated covers made of what appears to be silk or satin fabric call to me from the upper shelves, but I'd need a ladder. I see one several shelves over, built of gleaming mahogany with a smooth finish that matches the shelves, but I'd have to pull it over this way on its delicate looking wheels. Visions of it derailing and falling in my arms, smashing into the lower shelves, have me quickly changing my mind.

Instead, I step over to the nearest lower shelf and run my fingers over the smooth, cool wood. While I'd love to pluck a book off a shelf and dig through it, on second thought, I need to be careful. These books are so old, I'd probably need gloves to prevent any damage to the pages.

"I thought I'd find you here."

I jump like a child who's been caught with her hand in the cookie jar, spinning around to see the warm smile on Aunt Ida's face. I hadn't even heard her open the door.

"It's quite all right, dear," she says, still smiling. "I simply mean that it's only natural that the language arts teacher in the family would be curious about the library."

I exhale with relief. "I was hoping you wouldn't mind. I'm fascinated by literature, especially books this old and so well taken care of. This place is extraordinary."

She walks over to me, her smile meeting her blue eyes. "Of course I don't mind. In fact, I was hoping one of you young people would take an interest in the collection. It was so dear to Arthur... and to me."

"I can see that. You've taken great lengths to store it properly."

She nods gently. "Arthur insisted that the library maintain the proper temperature and humidity to preserve the books. And of course, the lights are low, so the paper doesn't yellow."

"It's quite clear how much the books meant to him." I glance back at the shelf. "I was just making a hopeless attempt to choose one to read—with gloves of course."

Aunt Ida chuckles and lifts her finger. "I think I have just the thing." She steps over to another bookshelf just beyond this one and takes out a huge tome, pages of different sizes sticking out from the leather binding. Her back bends against its weight.

"Let me help," I say. She hands it to me with a grateful smile, and I carry it over to one of the desks, where she flicks on the reading light.

"This is Arthur's Bunker Hill scrapbook," she explains as she scoots her chair to the side, leaving me room to pull up another chair before we sit. "If you want to know about the history of this house and the surrounding area, this is the best place to start. Your great-uncle loved history, especially as it related to this place. He collected everything he could find, papers, clippings, etc., about the local battles and the people here."

"This is amazing." I run my finger over the leather. "But I'm afraid to open it. Won't all this fall out?"

"If it does, we'll put it back together, dear," she assures me. "The knowledge in these pages was meant to be read."

Despite her reassurances, I open the book gingerly, still wishing I had gloves, and gritting my teeth as the binding crackles. But it stays intact as she shows me the first page.

"These are Monroe family records," she explains. "The family members who lived in this house back then were very proud of their contribution to the war effort. Two of the people who lived here actually fought in the Battle of Bunker Hill. Of course, being so close to the action, it's not surprising."

"That's fascinating." A vision of the wedding portrait enters my mind. Those were the parents who waited in fear to hear if their children would survive the battle, I'm guessing. I squint at the stylized handwriting.

"These are mostly from various acquaintances of the Monroes who sent back information about the battles." Her eyes twinkle with excitement as she flips through them slowly. "There was some element of danger sending these letters. They had to be passed through trusted hands."

"I can understand that. It must have been terrifying to go against the king. Even though they were a whole ocean away from him specifically, so many loyalists continued to work against the patriots until the very end of the war."

She nods, a hum escaping her pursed lips. "Here are some letters that mention members of the surrounding families. Several of the neighbors had men who fought in the battle as well."

Skimming the page, I notice the date, and my eyebrows arch. "June 17, 1775—that's almost exactly two hundred fifty years ago." I'd known the year, of course, but I'd never really studied the battle before and hadn't realized it happened in June.

Aunt Ida nods with a twinkle in her eye and carefully flips through a few more pages. "Ah, here it is."

An involuntary squeak escapes my lips when she lifts a piece of paper right off the page.

She lets out a chuckle. "It's okay. I didn't damage it."

Still, my hands go up in protest when she tries to give the paper to me. "I can't touch that."

Her mouth curls into a crooked grin. "Hattie, if you're going to sneak out tonight and go ghost hunting, I don't want you to get lost."

How does she know what I plan to do tonight? Heat rises in my cheeks as I look down at the paper. It's a small, hand-drawn map of the property and surrounding lands, including the area designated as the Thomas family property.

When my eyes finally meet hers again, she gives me a wink, which makes me blush even harder. She must have overheard me talking to Nina at dinner. I was trying to be so quiet….

"I can't take this," I tell her, trying to push her hand away.

But she doesn't budge. "I do think this will come in handy," she insists.

"This is a family heirloom." I nod toward the giant scrapbook. "I don't want to be the one who ruins it."

"You won't ruin anything." She smiles. "This map isn't that old."

"It's not?"

"My Arthur liked to draw maps," she continues. "He enjoyed considering alternative outcomes to what happened at Bunker Hill. He always insisted the battle could have been won by the colonists had they known how many British troops were there and how they would attack." She shakes her head, amusement dancing in her eyes. "My husband could spend hours arguing with his friends about how they would've done it differently had they been alive at the time. It brought him such joy."

"But this is a map of the property." I frown as I look at Aunt Ida then back at the map.

"Turn it over, dear."

Flipping the paper, I see a drawing of two hills, labeled 'Bunker' and 'Breed's.'

"The colonists had control of Boston only by land," she explains. "That river was filled with British ships, so they couldn't get control of the city from the waterways." Her eyes turn sullen as she gazes at the map. "Though the British won the battle, it cost them dearly and made them realize that the colonists were not people they could trifle with. Arthur loved the idea of the underdogs getting the upper hand, though he was always upset that it had to cost so many lives."

I nod grimly, imagining the fear of the couple in the portrait waiting for their sons to return from battle… or not.

"Anyway, your uncle had some ideas that might've changed

history if only the information had gotten into the right hands." She sighs, and her smile grows weary. It's clear she's beginning to run out of steam.

"This is very interesting," I tell her, still looking over the map.

"I'd better go get some rest," she says, her chair squeaking as she pushes it back. I rise as well, but she puts a hand on my shoulder. "There's no need for you to stop exploring the library. You're welcome to any books you'd like to read."

I glance at the ladder, and she lets out a chuckle. "I assure you, it's quite sturdy. Don't be afraid to use it if you want to read some of the books on the upper shelves."

"I would love that."

She smiles and pats my shoulder a few times before backing away. "More books about the battle are kept over there, where I got the scrapbook." She gazes at it, still open to the page where she took out the map. "And of course, Arthur's scrapbook has a wealth of information. If you're interested in the history of this place, you've come to the right place to learn. I know Uncle Arthur would be proud to see his legacy living on in you." She gazes at me with a knowing smile that leaves me wondering what else I'll discover in those pages.

"Goodnight, Aunt Ida." I smile back at her, my fingers itching to dig through more of the scrapbook.

"Goodnight, Hattie," she says. "Enjoy the library. Please think of it as your own. You're a Monroe, after all."

"Thank you," I tell her as she steps out the door.

Alone again, I eye those beautiful books on the top shelves and consider pulling the ladder out to get them. But something about Great Uncle Arthur's scrapbook tugs at my heart. I'm even more curious about the battle after glancing through the few letters I've already seen.

Looking down, I realize I'm still holding the map. A light chill passes over me, along with an odd feeling that I will need this piece of paper soon. There's no reason I'd need Arthur's Bunker Hill drawings, but the property map might come in handy if my phone loses signal while I'm out there alone tonight.

I fold it gently, only as many times as necessary to fit it in my pocket behind my phone. Then, I walk over to the bookshelves where Aunt Ida said the books about the battle were kept. I pursue them for a moment before piling up as many books about the Battle of Bunker Hill as I can fit in my arms and carrying them back to the table.

The scrapbook continues to intrigue me, so I flip a few more pages and read the letters and articles before studying the battle itself for a few hours before I decide I need to head out on my exploration.

I close the scrapbook and take a deep breath. All of this seems so personal now, as if I am slowly becoming a part of the battle itself. Knowing some of my own family members and their neighbors were entrenched in what was happening in the nation at the time makes it even more important to me.

I think about the man I think I saw earlier near the house. I try to imagine what his face might look like. Will I see him again? Eric Thomas, the man who built the cottage, died in that battle.

Is that who I saw? I hope to find out soon.

CHAPTER FOUR

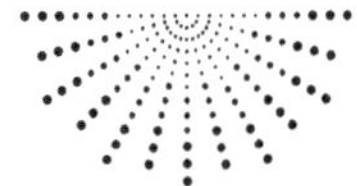

Hattie

"I can't believe you're going out there this late." Nina is still awake when I slip back into our room to gather up a few items I may need–like a flashlight. "Say hi to the ghosts for me."

I let out a chuckle and double-check the charge on my phone since I might need it if I get lost. "If I see a ghost, I won't be sticking around to tell it anything," I insist, though that's not completely true. If I see that man with the dark hair again, I'll know he's a ghost and not a figment of my imagination, and I just might work up the nerve to speak to him. There's just something about the cottage that makes me think it must be an interesting place at night."

"Well, you have fun with that." She flips over to face away from me and gives her pillow a few slaps while I stand here chuckling.

"Goodnight, Nina. If you're asleep when I get back, I'll see you in the morning."

"Goodnight!" She raises her arm from under the covers with a wave then snuggles up again.

I'm still giggling—quietly—when I place my hand on the banister and slip down the stairs. The bottom step creaks loudly in the eerie silence.

"Hattie?"

My heart lurches into my throat for a second until I recognize the figure on the landing. Taking a deep breath, I try to calm down. "Mom, I thought you were in bed already."

"I was." She sighs, descending the stairs to join me. "But I can't sleep."

"You really should try. You've been here for weeks helping take care of Uncle Arthur."

"A little herbal tea will help," she says. "Walk with me."

We make our way through the parlor on the way to the kitchen, and I admire the furnishings again as we pass. "It's like this place is frozen in time, isn't it?"

She shrugs, pushing through the double doors. "It is, in a way. And I'm guessing that's what has you wandering around it in the dark. Tea?"

"Yes, thanks." I have plenty of time to get out to the cottage, but I haven't had much of a chance to talk to Mom since I arrived.

She pours water into a stainless-steel teapot, lighting the modern gas stove, which oddly doesn't look out of place despite so much of the rest of the room dating back centuries. "Were you heading out?" She inclines her head toward the flashlight I set on the counter.

"Yes. To the cottage," I explain, leaning against the counter next to her.

"The little one that belongs to the Thomases?"

Nodding, I turn to snatch two tea bags out of the high cupboard. "Yes. It has me curious."

She looks at me, her eyes narrowed. "About what?"

With a deep breath, I pull two mugs from the cabinet and put the tea bags in them. "I don't know. We went and saw it earlier, and I thought I saw something. I need to go out there in the dark and see if I see it again."

"Are you saying you saw a ghost?" Mom's eyebrows raise, and a small smile of amusement forms on her lips.

"Maybe." I set the teacups down on the small kitchen table. "It was just for a split second. Then he was gone."

"He?"

"Yes, a man with dark hair in the forest," I explain.

"You've been interested in things like that ever since you were a kid. You were so sure you saw that girl on the side of the road." She smiles at me over her shoulder then turns back to the tea.

"Because I did see her," I insist. "It was pouring rain, and she was out there in a white dress. It can't be a coincidence that a newlywed couple died in a car accident right there."

"I believe you," she assures me. "I always have. But what's so special about this ghost?"

"I don't know." The whistling steam on the stove almost has me jumping out of my skin. Giggling at me, Mom lifts the teapot and brings it over. "It's this whole place, really. I want to know more about it, especially that cabin out there that no one has ever lived in."

"I was always curious about it myself," she admits, pouring our tea before returning the teapot and sitting with me, dunking her tea bag in the steaming water. "But I never saw any ghosts."

"I just need to know if it's all related."

We chat a while longer until our teacups are empty. "Well, I'd better try to get some sleep," she says. "Don't stay out there too late, and be sure you have your phone with you."

"I do." I slide it out of my pocket. "It's fully charged."

"I expect a full briefing about the ghost in the morning." She smiles in a teasing way that's also full of love.

I chuckle. "You've got it." She steps out of the kitchen with a wave.

After giving the cups a quick wash, I finally make my way toward the back door that opens to a stone patio. Inhaling a deep breath to feel the fresh summer air in my lungs, I gaze up at the stars above, many of them faded against the waning gibbous moon. Crickets chirp from the tall grass edging the property, filling the air with the song of the night. Exhaling, I look to the south and begin my walk back to the cottage.

Off the patio, the well-kept lawn eventually gives way to the forest. It's sparse at first, but the massive tree trunks are soon partially obscured by bushes and underbrush, though there are several paths leading partway through.

It's so dark, I'm having trouble remembering exactly which way I went with Nina and my cousins, so I get the compass working on my phone, the beam of the flashlight illuminating the path in front of me. I take note of the moon's position and head south. It's more difficult to navigate now, and occasionally I find myself stumbling over a root or running into a particularly long branch of a bush.

As I get deeper into the forest, I lose some of the moonlight to the thick canopy above me, and I start to hear more sounds of the forest. My feet crunch through dry leaves, and something scampers off into the darkness. I shine my flashlight after it, wondering if it's the ghost again, but I don't see anything, and it seemed to be more the size of a small animal than a man.

Continuing forward, I do a better job of keeping my light on the ground so I don't trip over another root and face plant. I have to admit, Nina's jokes about breaking a leg aren't too far-fetched given all the roots and branches littering the forest floor.

Finally, I step through the forest into the clearing around the cottage, finding myself almost exactly where we'd come through earlier. The scene under the moonlight is breathtaking, the soft glow reflecting off the cottage's stone exterior, muting the brownish red color that had been so vibrant in the evening light. Its presence is still commanding, even though the dwelling itself is not that large, especially compared to Aunt Ida's home.

Stepping onto the porch, I feel compelled to touch the stone again and admire its construction. It's a marvel that one man built this practically on his own with rudimentary materials. The uneven sizes of stones seem to perfectly fit together like a giant puzzle. There are no gaps in mortar, even after all these years, with no sign of patching and repair by the Thomas family like I'd seen in the replaced window and porch railing. I wish I could go inside, but I'm sure it's still locked up tight.

Figuring the mystery man—or ghost—might reappear in the same place I first spotted him, I make myself comfortable on the porch step. A soft summer breeze passes over the forest canopy and down into the little cottage yard, giving me a chill that makes me fold my arms across my stomach, even though it's a fairly warm June night.

Inhaling, I close my eyes, listening intently to the forest's song. An owl hoots far off in the distance. Further still, a dog barks at something, his tone deep, likely a large breed.

Hoping to catch sight of the man or maybe some other ghost, I open my eyes quickly like I did earlier, darting my gaze over to the trees where I'd seen him before.

But I don't see anything ghostlike at all.

Maybe I'll have better luck in the backyard.

In the backyard, I pass the old well and its fragile grate that definitely needs replacement. I wonder why the Thomas family hasn't fixed that yet. Shrugging, I pass by it, making a note to go a different direction so I don't end up with an "I told you so" from Nina if I accidentally fall in. God, that would be awful.

A giant tree stands to the right on the edge of the back yard. This one looks even older than the others. It's so large, with gnarled roots that stick out from the ground. Intrigued by its enchanting nature, I wander over to the tree and sit down between two of the over-sized roots with my back against the trunk and stare at the little cottage illuminated by the moonlight. If I'm still and quiet, maybe the ghost will make another appearance.

Rustling noises from a bush next to me have my head turning on a swivel. I wait for a moment, holding my breath, but nothing emerges, so I assume it's just another animal scrounging around for something to eat.

I settle back against the tree trunk, and my mind wanders to the stories I read in Uncle Arthur's scrapbook. Visions of war torn battlefields, rivers of blood flowing between shattered bodies, smoke billowing past like low lying clouds come to mind. So many people lost their lives here. An entire battalion of ghosts could march out of these trees at any moment.

Maybe I shouldn't be here after all. I glance over my shoulder, thinking I see something out of the corner of my eye, but there's nothing there. I take a deep breath and tell myself I'm being silly. I'm most likely not gonna see another ghost, certainly not a mass of them all at once.

I stifle a yawn. Drinking that herbal tea before I came out here was probably a big mistake. I'm starting to feel drowsy. Being half asleep stumbling through a strange forest at night probably isn't the best idea. It might be time for me to give up the ghost hunt and go home.

A bit disappointed that I didn't get to see the man from earlier again, I haul myself up to my feet. Out of the corner of my eye, I see a flash of movement and turn in that direction, casting the flashlight beam over toward a cluster of bushes.

Nothing.

I take a deep breath, but my heart continues to hammer against my ribcage. An eerie feeling sets in. Slowly, I turn in a circle, the weight of unseen eyes bearing down on me.

The flashlight beam coasts over something I hadn't noticed before. Not far away from the tree where I've been sitting, a large, flat stone lies on the ground. It looks like someone intentionally placed it there, not like it's naturally occurring. I didn't notice it last time I was here, though I really hadn't spent much time in the backyard.

Still keeping an eye on my surroundings, I walk over to it, squat down, and touch it. It's warm, probably from being in the hot summer sun all day. At first, I think it might be a discarded stone that was too big to use in its construction, but when I sweep the dirt off it, I find that's not the case. It's too dark to be made of sandstone, too heavy.

But there's something on it, indentations on the surface that I can feel. Shining my light directly on its surface, I can see that something is written there. I brush away more dirt to get a better look.

Once again, I find myself breathless as I gaze down at a name carved into the stone.

Eric.

As if shocked by an electric current, I fall backward onto my bottom before scrambling to my feet. My muscles tense, and I look around and quickly determine I definitely don't want to be here alone anymore. I shiver as a chill rises up my back, and I rub my arms, goosebumps forming under my fingers. It's one thing to stand here and admire a two-hundred-fifty-year-old house. But it's quite another to find an old rock in the dark and run my fingers over the homeowner's name.

This is just way too creepy.

Out of nowhere, a screech, something like a banshee's yell, hits my ears. I spin around in the dark, looking wide-eyed into the dark trees. A giant owl flutters from one tree to another, spreading its wings and almost flying right over my head.

Okay, that's it. I'm out of here.

I should have listened to Nina and just gone to bed, putting this whole thing behind me. Why did I insist on coming out here at night? When she said she refused to come, why didn't I just forget about the idea? I'm an idiot for coming out here alone.

Not that I feel like I'm alone….

With my heart thumping wildly in my chest, I turn and run into the darkness. I'm not sure which way to go, but my mind tells me I need to get to the front yard, back to the path, right now.

Another noise sounds behind me. I tell myself it's just that damn owl again, but I spin around so quickly, my phone slips from my grasp. My foot hits something sharp, but I can't focus on the pain right now. I don't see anything else, but every hair on my body is standing on end.

"Let's go home," I say aloud to myself, afraid to turn my back on the forest. I take a deep breath and spin around to walk toward the front yard again.

That's when I realize what I caught my foot on.

The grate over the well!

I take another step–and there's no ground beneath my foot. I must've kicked the fragile old grate away from the hole. I'm moving too quickly to stop my forward momentum. The next thing I know, there's nothing below me but empty air.

Dropping the flashlight, I desperately try to cling to the smooth rock sides as I fall, kicking frantically, trying to gain some traction, but nothing's working.

Time stands still. It feels like I'm falling for miles. Still fighting to keep from plummeting, I whirl around frantically, hitting my head on the side of the well. Pain radiates through my skull. I lift a hand and feel a sticky substance coating my palm, but a moment later, I find myself plummeting underwater. Cold, murky water fills my lungs. I fight to rise to the surface, to get a breath of air, but I fell so far down, it takes forever for me to finally reach the top again. When my mouth finally comes above the top of the water, I suck in some air, but my whole body hurts, and stars are beginning to take over my field of vision.

Above me, I see a small sliver of moonlight. And then… complete darkness.

CHAPTER FIVE

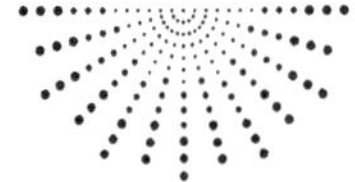

HATTIE

THE WORLD SPINS FOR A FEW MINUTES, AND A SHARP THROB IN THE BACK of my head radiates toward my eyes. Through my closed eyelids, the world seems too bright for a well of this depth, and the idea that I should be sinking in a bottomless well has my eyes flying open.

But there's no water–only air. And a gritty, earthy taste in my mouth.

This isn't right. Where's the water?

Spitting frantically, I look up just in time to see a clump of dirt falling toward me. I shield my eyes and move toward the side of the hole.

"Help!" My parched throat barely emits a sound.

"Keep at it. I'll be but a moment."

Who the hell is that?

Another lump of dirt falls on me.

"Hey!"

The barrage stops, but I purse my lips in anger and brush the dust off my face. "Nina! Harry! Help!"

No, that's wrong. Nina and Harry didn't come out here with me.

Soft rays of sunshine beam into the hole. Is it morning already? I look around at the hole around me... and it's solid, without a drop of water.

What the hell?

My head is throbbing. I keep a hand pressed to the back where I'm certain I hit the stones lining the well when I fell. Stones that are no longer here. Blinking, I struggle to focus. I should be underwater. None of this makes sense.

"Is someone down there?"

I open my mouth to cry out again, but I stop mid-word. That's not Nina... or my mom. "Who's there?" I ask.

A girl peeks over the edge of the wall above me, wisps of her auburn hair swaying in front of her eyes. *Why isn't the wall made of stone?* "Grace of God, there's a woman in there," the girl says. "One moment, miss!"

She disappears from the top of the hole, and I push myself up to my tiptoes, but the top of the hole is just high enough that I can't reach the ledge. That's not right either. I remember falling several yards before even hitting the water.

Moments later, a roughly tied rope lands against the wall.

"Grab hold, miss!"

It's hard to get a grip on the coarse, partially frayed rope, but I manage to get a loop around my hand before I feel it being tugged.

"Pull, everyone!" the girl hollers.

After a moment, I manage to get my arm, then one knee, up on the ledge and roll away from the hole, finding myself surrounded by a group of kids, most quite a bit younger than the girl who'd called down to me. Every one of them is wearing colonial clothes, much like those I've seen in portraits throughout the Monroe estate. Bewilderment fills their eyes as they all stare at me in silence, jaws open.

"Where... what's happening?" I ask.

The auburn-haired girl crinkles her brow and tucks loose strands of hair into her bonnet. She stands about an inch taller than me, though judging by her features, she can't be much older than my students, seventeen or eighteen at most. Her posture is erect and confident, and her sky-blue eyes gaze at me with curiosity. "Happening? I fear I don't understand," she says.

I'm sure I look just as confused as she does. *Why are they wearing these clothes?*

The girl moves closer, her slender face examining me head to toe. "How did you come to be in that hole?" she asks, but I have no time to answer before more questions spill from her lips. "Who are you? From whence do you come? "

It's only now that I hear her accent clearly—British, sort of, but with a regional dialect I've never heard before. "I'm Hattie Miller, from Seattle," I explain, my throbbing head keeping my thoughts from flowing clearly.

"What is Seattle?"

I tilt my head in confusion and answer her other question. "I'm not sure how I got into this hole. I fell into your well and—"

"But that cannot be," she argues, her head shaking back and forth furiously. "The men have only just struck water. They're off to seek help building the well."

"Let's start over," I suggest. I try to sit up, but my head won't allow me to. "I'm Hattie. What's your name?"

"Charlie Monroe, and the children are my brothers and sisters."

My spine tingles as I realize the striking similarity between these kids and all the portraits I've seen in the house, especially the one little girl whose red hair is a perfect match for my shade. I turn to her, meeting eyes just like mine, a couple of degrees darker than her older sister's, and lean toward her height. "What's your name?" I ask.

"Penelope," she answers, but then she slips behind Charlie, turning away.

I try to smile through the pain, holding my head. The throbbing is seeming to let up a little, and my vision is becoming clearer.

"My sister is timid," Charlie explains. "This is Matthew, Clayton, and Elizabeth."

"Hello," I say with a nod at each of them. Elizabeth gives me a small, charming smile, familiar dimples creasing in her cheeks.

Turning, I lift my hand over my mouth to hold in a gasp. The house beside me has no windows, no front door, not even the charming stone porch. Yet, it's the same cottage. There's no mistaking its solid stone construction.

What the hell is happening?

I turn to get my bearings. The hole I just crawled out of is just that —an empty hole. Next to it sits another one, but it's not even half as deep as the well I fell into, and there's no smooth sandstone walls in either of them.

A shiver goes down my spine. *What is this place?* The trees around me are smaller, including the grand white oak I leaned against as I waited for the ghost, its protruding roots smaller and its truck thinner.

Maybe I'm not where I think I am.

Maybe somehow, for some reason, I fell into the well and ended up back in time. That sounds ridiculous, but...

How hard did I hit my head?

I'm sitting by the cottage before it is even completed. But how can that be? I fold my arms under my chest, gazing in turn at the house, the hole, these children, and the dirt on my clothes.

How the hell did this happen? And why?

Charlie steps closer to me. "Are you well, miss?"

I turn to her and try to speak, but all my words get caught up in my throat. Her eyes soften, and she reaches out to take my hand.

"I don't know how you managed to stumble across our property and fall into that hole while we were standing right there, but Mother always says to lend a helping hand whenever we can. We'd best get you cleaned up before the men see you like this."

All I can do is nod as she addresses the kids.

"Sit here, and dare not think of scattering until John and Eric return."

Eric—Eric Thomas. She knows him?

I didn't find his ghost, but I must be back in time when he was still finishing his cottage....

I'm aware of a gentle tug from Charlie as she pulls my hand. I manage to get to my feet, staying away from the holes.

We move toward the forest. Its trees and bushes are similar to what I walked through in the night, yet now there's a cleared path leading through it. I shoot one last glance over my shoulder before the cottage disappears from view.

Is this real?

"I don't really know what's happening," I mutter, the pain in my head subsiding but my confusion continuing. "That house–who did you say it belongs to?" *Am I dreaming?*

"The man who owns the property is called Eric Thomas."

I turn to face her. I did hear her correctly. She still holds my hand firmly as we walk down the path, quicker now since I'm beginning to keep up.

"He went with some other men to fetch more shovels," she continues. "Earlier, he found the underground creek which will be perfect for the well's location."

Now that I've had a moment to think about it, I still can't fathom how I'm in the past. Maybe the windows were there, but the sun was hitting the cottage wrong. And maybe someone was digging a new well. That old one was dangerous, after all.

That doesn't explain the children, their clothing, or their strange speech–but there has to be another logical explanation, doesn't there?

"Why were you throwing the dirt in?" I ask.

"Eric asked us to," she explains. "He wished us to cover the unnecessary holes… lest someone fall in," she explains, shaking her head. "I never once stepped away from the hole. I do not understand how you came to be in there."

"I honestly don't know either," I tell her.

She stops walking, her eyes intent as she looks into mine. After a moment, she gives me a dimpled smile. "We'll get you cleaned up and tend to your wound, then perhaps your thoughts will clear."

Nodding, I follow as she pulls me along again. *I hope she's right.*

There's something calming about the forest, even when I'm feeling so confused and my head is still aching. I try to stop thinking about the possibility of being in another century. Birds sing cheerfully, and the sparse canopy allows the warm sunlight through. Charlie drops my hand, and I brush off the mess of dust on my jeans the best I can while we continue forward.

She picks up the pace. "At this hour, we'll likely avoid the servants if we hurry. We'll want to steer clear of the housekeeper, Catherine, particularly. She's already warned against trailing a mess into the house, knowing we were going down to the build site."

It occurs to me that she's taking a risk bringing me, a stranger, into her home. "Are you sure your parents won't mind that I'm in your house?"

She shakes her head. "To care for one in need? Never. You are in need, are you not?"

"Yes, I suppose I am." After all, I have no other resources wherever the hell I am—or whenever. "Thank you."

She returns my smile, and we continue along the path, the wild bushes fading into a trimmed hedge on either side.

This kind, helpful girl has me curious. "Charlie is an unusual name."

She breathes out the sigh of a person who has been questioned many times before. "Charlotte is my given name. I prefer Charlie."

"It suits you."

She stops, turns to me, and looks into my eyes for a moment. "My thanks to you. Not many feel the same." The grunt she lets out at the end tells me she's fed up with being told what to do.

I like this girl already.

"Here we are."

I inhale sharply as we reach the back of the massive Monroe estate. Its strong rock walls stand just as regal as I remember, though the patio is paved in bricks, and the three large air conditioning units are missing from the side. The window glass is thicker, and the back door has a heavier wood frame.

My muscles tense as reality hits me. There's no other explanation for this. The well, cottage, the trees, and now the house....

This is real. I'm in the past.

"Allow me a moment," she says at the back door.

I nod, still mulling over my situation while she pulls the door open and moves cautiously inside, returning a moment later to wave me in. I find my senses again and follow her, stepping inside the original edification of the Monroe estate—in what looks to be centuries earlier than I'd left it only a few hours before. A chill rushes over me when I look up at the wooden archways, so beautiful, so unnervingly familiar.

It takes all my energy to keep up with Charlie, and I'm glad for the distraction. We stride quickly toward the stairway, though I catch a quick glimpse of the parlor along the way. Aunt Ida's favorite chair is still there, but the sofa looks unfamiliar. I suppose this one didn't survive the centuries.

What does remain is the smooth mahogany banister, which I grab hold of before stepping on the first stair, only to find it solid, without a single creak.

With so many rooms on the second floor, I'm surprised when Charlie takes me in a familiar direction, directly to the room I've been sharing with Nina.

Gazing around it, I can't help but smile. The only difference I can see is pink floral wallpaper instead of paint.

But the reminder of my sister makes my breath catch in my lungs. I press a hand to my chest to steady myself. I don't know how I got here, or how such a thing is even possible. I whip my head around, every inch of my body tensed, ready to run. Fight or flight mode is kicking in. But even if I run out of this room, this house, or miles through the forest, I'll still be years away from everyone I know and love.

I got here through the well, but it doesn't even exist yet.

What if I can't ever go back?

CHAPTER SIX

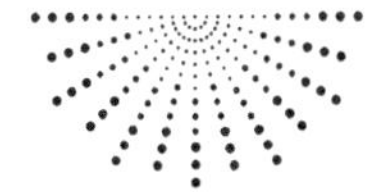

"It's quite a stroke of luck how quickly we've hit water." My friend and neighbor, John, pauses to take a sip from our canteen, wiping his brow with the bottom of his shirt, clearing away a streak of dirt from his tan skin.

"T'was no luck about it," I argue. "I spent many a midafternoon calculating the likely trajectory of the underground creek before I raised a single cornerstone."

"I jest," he admits. "No one has the forethought of such matters quite like you."

"And none carries a load of rock so well as you." I compliment my friend with ease. He was the first to offer his assistance when I suggested building the home. We sat together at the time in this very spot in the forest between our families' estates, near the location where we are building my cottage, musing for endless hours about our future wives, families, and occupations. It is the very place where we worked out our childhood fancies through playful warfare, long before the British conflict had us side by side on a bloody battlefield.

During the battle, he cared not only for his own safety, but mine. When a Redcoat advanced unexpectedly toward me, my oldest friend grabbed hold of my shoulder to pull me behind a boulder to safety. It is I who should carry rocks for him, a thousand times over. Yet, he does so for me with an easy smile.

My brother Colin brushes back his blond hair as we walk across the meadow, and I turn to him. Such a change I have seen in him since the battle. His face is still youthful, but his demeanor is confident, poised. His eyes, once full of fire, gaze out at the world with quiet depth, having now seen far too many of its faults. He gazes at me with the same chocolate brown eyes I see when I look in the mirror, though his are a bit more suspicious of the world than they used to be. "Perhaps we could get on to the stables."

"Aye," I say softly. Only two years my junior at twenty-one, he is loath to admit in front of the others how painful it is to remain long on his feet. The shrapnel at Concord grazed just above his ankle. Thankfully, it didn't protrude too deeply, yet the ache persists.

The others follow as we approach my family's stable. "You can make ready the brown mare," I tell John, retrieving my saddle from the brass hook by the entry. My brothers, and the neighbors who have joined in my well project, Richard and Isaac, disburse to fetch their steeds.

John gives a wave to the groom, Elias. "Still a bucker, is she?" John asks him.

"Aye, but she seems to have a soft spot for 'ye," he retorts.

I smile at the interaction, making my way over to my black Saddlebred.

My brother, Levi, follows me and prepares his favorite horse in the stall next to mine. "Do you still intend to gift the mare to your future bride?" he asks as we lead them out.

"I do."

"'Tis hardly time to speak of marriage and gifts when war threatens," Colin warns from the paddock outside, where Elias assists him into his saddle.

"Do you believe it would be so soon?" Levi asks. "You are injured yet."

Colin turns to our brother with a furrowed brow. "The call of freedom waits not for injuries," he insists. "My wound but heightens my disdain for British rule."

My stomach churns at the topic. "Freedom we will acquire, but for now, we have need of shovels and muscle."

"Aye," John agrees. "Perhaps we must seek the Robinson men. The lads are strong, and their equipment is in good supply."

"To the Robinson estate then." With a flick of my wrist, my mare trots forward through the paddock gate Elias holds open. My brothers and John ride at my side, while Richard and Isaac follow.

The morning sun brightens the deep blue sky, obstructed only by occasional billowing clouds. The peaceful scene causes my mind to wander. While 'tis true war is the topic at hand, eventually, I'd like to find a marriageable woman with whom I feel the pull of romance, despite my mother's persistence at unsubtle introductions. I don't fault her impatience, for I feel it myself, longing to settle into married life with a woman I love. Perhaps providence waits for the completion of the home we'll share together, and the end of this war.

"Tell me again. Why are you not betrothed to the Williams girl?"

John's unexpected inquiry has me turning my head. My mouth opens, but my speech is interrupted when Colin answers for me. "Our brother seeks more than a lovely face."

"She is from a fine family," Levi chimes in. "As eldest, should your wife not be well connected?"

"Suitability as a wife depends not on connections," Colin tells him.

"And yet–" Levi begins, but I raise a hand to interrupt.

"I shall decide who will be a suitable wife for myself," I assert. "The Williams girl is pleasing to the eye, yet I feel no attraction toward her."

"How could you not, with that honey blonde hair and those striking emerald orbs?" Levi's hazel eyes regard me, and I'm beginning to think perhaps he should be the one marrying the Williams girl. I lift my shoulders in a shrug. "Those green eyes gaze at me with emptiness. I prefer a well-read woman, one with an opinion of her own, and a sharp mind full of reason."

"The Jones girl is intelligent," Colin suggests.

I nod. "This is true, yet no feelings of love move between us."

"Eric is a man of romance," John chimes in. "When the right woman is before him, I have no doubt he will recognize it."

I give my friend a smile for his support. How often I have admitted to him that I cannot marry without true love and friendship with the woman I choose.

Levi shakes his head. "I do not understand your insistence on love and romance."

"And yet it sounds like you may well be in love with the Williams girl yourself." That gets a chuckle out of everyone. Even Levi, who turns a bit pink in the cheeks but doesn't disagree. "When you are of marriageable age, perhaps you will be pleased that the choice is purely yours," I suggest.

"And then, perhaps, I shall build my own cottage," Levi says with a nod.

"Perhaps you shall," I agree. "There is yet time to build a similar cottage by your own hand. Our property is vast. You might consider positioning yours by the rear property line."

"Perhaps I will."

I let out a laugh. At seventeen, he is of age to fight in the militia and held his own in the recent battles at Lexington and Concord, thankfully. Yet, his childish stubbornness often surfaces.

"Levi, even our dear brother may find his home construction post-poned by the war," Colin warns. "There is much talk of future battles among our neighbors."

Levi turns his lips down in a frown. "Do you think we'll be called again soon?"

"It's inevitable," John says, his legs tensing as he guides the horse beneath him. He turns to Levi. "The last battle leaves British rule impossible to bear. I shall be proud to serve the Massachusetts Provincial Congress in our charge for freedom."

"As will I," I say with a nod. "It's clear in my mind the provinces in the Americas can no longer abide being British colonies. I will stand by my brothers and neighbors to fight for our lives and futures."

"And we shall all do the same," Colin states firmly.

"Although my devotion to this cause is strong, even mere talk of war leaves a bitter taste in my mouth when the peace of family life feels so near to me," I continue. "Knowing our time at home is but a short reprieve from battle unsettles me, though I am thankful the militia allows for such a break."

"We shall be victorious, and that peace shall be even more prosperous," John assures me.

"I pray it will," I say solemnly. I turn my gaze to Colin's injured leg, and an ache forms in my gut. "At what cost will we find liberty? We've few casualties compared with many families who sent sons to battle. Will our good fortune hold?" Icy chills crawl up my spine at the thought.

"I am well, brother," Colin says. "Worry not."

"Worry is not abated by words," I reply.

"Aye, we will continue to worry for those we love," John agrees. "I'll not look forward to watching after Charlie again." I turn to him and regard his grim expression. He shakes his head at the recent memory. "She was fortunate not to be caught in the center of battle. Had I known she'd followed us, I would have turned her back more swiftly."

"It was a blessing Levi spotted her," I reply.

Levi nods. "I very nearly did not recognize her in that manner of dress."

"I'll keep a closer watch on my shirts and trousers, that is certain," John says. "My sister is quite unique. I won't deny her self-expression, but I will not permit harm to come to her. I draw the line at her participating in combat."

"As you should," I agree. Imagining the possible outcomes of that night still sends shivers through me. "It may be more taxing to keep her away if the next battle is close by."

"Do you expect as much?" John asks.

"I do." I cannot ignore the British ships surrounding the Boston peninsula, only a few short miles from our home. I've been troubled by an ache in my gut since their very arrival.

John's cheeks quiver as he exhales forcefully. "Your instincts are often correct. But location aside, I'm quite certain we'll be called back to service soon."

"I believe it will come quickly as well," Levi agrees.

"I remain at the ready, as should we all," Colin says somberly as we ride up to the Robinson estate.

"Has there been word regarding the war?" Nathaniel Robinson, who is working in the yard, asks as we approach his family home. His brother, George, stands beside him, his arms tense at his side.

"Nay," I reply. "We were speaking only of the likelihood of a battle one day soon."

"I doubt not," Nathaniel says. "I fear the heavy British approach by sea as they reenforce their ranks."

"As do I." I shake my head at the thought

"Can we rouse enough militia to match them?" Levi asks. "Our victory at Lexington and Concord surely has increased patriotism in our province."

"I believe it has, and I have confidence we shall have the men we need," John replies with a forceful nod.

Colin turns to the Robinsons. "Eric, supposes the fight will be near."

"Is it so?" Nathaniel turns to me, his brow raised.

I nod grimly. "I fear the Redcoats will take the fight inland from the peninsula."

"This is most grave." George runs a hand through his dark hair. "What of our families?"

"I believe it's best to plan for the protection of the women should the battle be close," Nathaniel suggests.

As the others agree, my heart quickens at the thought of my mother losing a single son, much less three. Though she would take comfort in the three young sons who remain, nothing can replace a lost child in the heart of a mother.

The thought has me struggling for breath. I cannot abide the fever in my heart at the thought of one of my brothers taking a fatal bullet.

"Nathaniel, our grandmother can scarcely descend the staircase, much yet run a household with ease." George's hands shake as he regards his brother. "Suppose something becomes of both of us?"

"Father will care for her," Nathaniel assures him.

"And my wife is with child," my neighbor Richard adds. "She and the little ones would be in dire need without me."

"We shall agree here to care for each other's families should the others perish," John suggests.

The group responds with grim nods. The ache in my gut grows heavy at the mention of our families left without sons and husbands. I long for a peaceful Massachusetts, where I may have the leisure to pursue a wife, a need that has grown strong in my heart since the first signs of colonial discontent. I wish to continue to build a home that ensures my future wife hasn't a care but the tending of our children and our home as well as any hobbies she may enjoy. How often I've imagined the happy scene in my dreams.

Yet, I am well aware that such tranquility comes at a price, and I am willing to answer the call with my life, if needed. The defense of my family and our property is my honored duty, though I'd prefer to use my hands to build a peaceful future rather than take life through war.

I gaze around at the others as they continue to arrange for care of each other's families. This grim topic leaves no room for intent to obtain shovels, at least for now. John regards me with sympathetic eyes, yet the others continue to speak of battle, strategy, and painful loss.

I want only to dig into the earth, to finish the well and continue work on my home. The inevitable call of war looms near, and I know not whether I shall ever experience the pleasure of finishing my home, the love of a woman, or the joy of carrying my child in my arms.

Now, I can only await the call to battle as the threat of doom approaches my doorstep.

"Enough of all this talk of war," John finally says, likely seeing my concern. "We have come to ask for shovels, and a hand in digging a well, should you gentlemen oblige."

"Yes, indeed," Nathaniel answers for both of them. "Let us move to happier topics. Eric Thomas has a house to build!"

I smile, and the men go about fetching their shovels and readying to come with us, but the shadow of war follows us still, wherever we go.

CHAPTER SEVEN

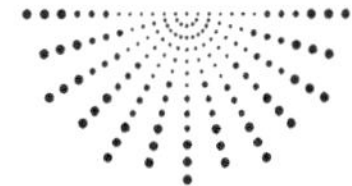

Hattie

MY FROZEN PANIC LINGERS AS CHARLIE MOVES TO THE OAK WARDROBE at the back of her room, flipping through the dresses on wooden hangers. She bombards me with questions, but I don't answer a single one. My mind is consumed with only one thought: How the hell do I get home?

"You say you're from Seattle," she says, her back to me. "I've never heard of such a place. Where is it? And you're a Miller, you say? Are you related to the Millers of Beacon Hill?"

I say nothing, but that doesn't deter her.

"I can't make sense of how you appeared so quickly in that hole," she continues, then turns toward me, her gaze narrowing. "Are you a British spy? Is that why you're wearing men's clothes?"

Her accusatory tone sends a chill through me. Before I know it, tears are streaming down my face. I just want to go home.

Charlie's expression softens immediately. "My apologies. I've been a terrible host. You need care, not accusations." She moves swiftly to a vanity drawer, pulling out a cloth and dipping it into a bowl of water resting on top. She carries it over to me along with a small silver-framed mirror.

We don't exchange words as she hands me the cloth. Her eyes are gentle, sympathetic, and I gratefully press the cool, damp fabric to my face. The streaks of dirt from my tears are obvious now, my face flushed and blotchy from crying. The cloth feels soothing against my skin. I take a deep breath, trying to ground myself.

Charlie quietly returns to the wardrobe, pulling out a dress and several folded items from drawers beneath the hanging items. She places them on one of the beds. After closing the wardrobe doors behind her, she gestures to my soiled clothes and hands me a simple cotton shift, turning her back to give me privacy.

I hesitate for only a moment before I start pulling off my shirt and wondering what to do with my old clothes that won't get dirt all over Charlie's room.

She holds out her hand behind her, and I hand over my shirt, which she takes without a word, folding them neatly before setting them aside on a chair. She does the same with my jeans, though she raises an eyebrow when she sees the condition of them.

Turning away, she dips the cloth back into the bowl of water, wrings it out, and hands it back to me so I can wipe away the dust and dirt from the rest of my body. Another cloth follows to dry me off.

Once I have the shift on, I let Charlie know. "You can turn around now, if you'd like. I may need some assistance."

"Of course." She helps me with the corset. Thankfully, she doesn't pull too tightly as she ties it then hands me a petticoat. I slide that on, and she helps me tie it. After that, a light blue dress styled like the ones I've seen in portraits of women from this era follows.

She gestures toward the vanity. "Let me help with your hair."

I sit obediently, my eyes widening when I catch sight of myself in the large, round mirror. For a moment, I think I look like one of the Monroes I'd seen in old pictures, though I don't know which one. Our family resemblance runs deep.

Charlie runs a pearl-handled brush gently through my hair, then lifts it into a bun, securing it with practiced hands. She twirls my natural curls around her fingers, arranging them just right so they dangle elegantly to frame my face.

"Thank you," I tell her. "For everything."

"Of course." She smiles at my reflection.

But now that I can no longer attempt to convince myself that I didn't somehow fall back in time, I have questions. "What's the date?" I blurt.

She pauses, still holding a curl in place. She meets my eyes in the mirror. "Why, today is Saturday, June tenth."

"Uhm, what year?"

"You must've hit your head harder than I realized," she replies, pulling her hand back and studying me with concern. "It's 1775, of course."

"I did hit my head," I admit. It still aches. "But that's not the problem." There's no denying it now. I'm stuck in 1775, just days before a pivotal battle in the Revolutionary War. I have no idea how to act or where to go, but Charlie seems willing to help. Maybe I don't have a choice but to trust her. "Can you keep a secret, Charlie?"

Her brows lift slightly, and she steps back, sitting on the edge of the bed behind me. "I can, provided you're not truly a British spy." A sly smile curves the corners of her lips.

I spin around to face her, shaking my head. "No, I'm not a spy."

She leans forward, eager. "I promise I won't tell."

"I'm from the future," I tell her before I can second-guess myself.

She tilts her head, confusion crossing her face.

I take a deep breath, my hands relaxing as I continue. "I'm from the year 2025. While my last name is Miller, I'm a Monroe by birth. My Great Uncle Arthur died, and my family came to visit my Great Aunt Ida, who lives here."

Charlie's brow furrows in disbelief. "How could this be?"

"I don't know," I admit. "But it's the only explanation that makes sense. I was curious about the cottage—the home Eric Thomas is building now—and I fell into the well. I hit my head, blacked out, and then... I woke up here with you."

She stands up suddenly, pacing the room, deep in thought. I sit in silence, waiting.

Finally, she stops and sits back on her bed, rubbing her chin.

"I guess I traveled back in time," I add, my voice unsure. "It's the only explanation."

"Is this common in... 2025?" she asks slowly.

"No," I answer, shaking my head. "Time travel is as impossible there as it is here. But it's what happened."

Charlie's eyes widen, then relax as she looks down at the quilt on her bed, thoughtfully tracing the flowers with her finger. "I should be more shocked, but... strangely, I am not."

"You believe me?" I ask, relief washing over me.

She nods, her gaze soft. "It's extraordinary, yes. But your unusual clothes, your sudden appearance—your manner of speech—it all fits with this revelation. To be honest, I would've been more suspicious had you not admitted you were from the future."

The weight of her acceptance finally hits me, and I blink away another tear. "I just... it's terrifying, actually."

Charlie stands and places a hand gently on my shoulder. "You are not alone here. We're family, are we not?"

I wipe the tear away, grateful for her kindness. "We are. Thank you—again."

"You're welcome, Hattie." She smiles. "I've always liked that name." But then, she frowns again. "You did injure your head when you fell, did you not?"

I nod. "Like I said, I hit my head, but it's feeling better now."

"That must've been a twenty-foot drop to the underground creek," she says. "I know, because I'm helping my brother with the well. My mother says it's unladylike, but I told her I'd just watch the construction. I have secrets, too."

"I can keep your secret if you can keep mine," I say with a small smile, though an ache settles in my stomach. This is going to be difficult. People are going to question who I am and how I got here.

"Do not worry," she says, offering a reassuring smile. "I will help you adjust."

I nod, knowing I'll need her more than ever. The sound of a clock striking the half hour drifts up from downstairs.

"My parents will be in the parlor for tea soon," she says, rising from the bed. "I'll need to speak with them about you. We'll need a story for where you've come from."

My heart is racing. "Maybe we can say something happened to my parents."

"That's a good idea," she agrees. "Perhaps your father was injured at Lexington and Concord."

I pause, trying to recall the specifics. "Lexington and Concord... right."

Charlie grins. "Good. We'll say you've lost both your parents and have nowhere to go. My mother and father would never turn away a young woman in need. I'm sure they'll have you share my room."

"You're right," I reply, grateful for her generosity. "Your parents sound wonderful."

"All Monroes are wonderful." She winks playfully.

I let out a soft giggle. It's the first time I've laughed since waking up in this strange place. The ache of missing my family still weighs heavily on me, but at least I have Charlie to help me navigate.

And... maybe I'll get to see Eric Thomas in the flesh.

CHAPTER EIGHT

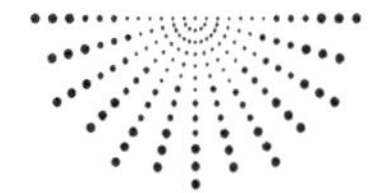

Eric

"It is fine news that my window glass will arrive soon," I tell everyone as we make our way to the cottage. "I'd feared it wouldn't arrive in time with so many shipments affected by the war."

"I was happy to assist in its acquisition," John says. "Luck was with us that the proper sizes had previously been delivered to my uncle's storehouse."

"Indeed." Joy fills my heart at the thought of completing my new home soon. While I consider the technique of their installation, we round the last turn toward the back of my cottage.

"Who is that strange woman with my sister?" John asks, his brows knitted together.

I follow his gaze. Beside his sister Charlie and their many younger siblings stands another woman, assisting Charlie with the shoveling. I catch a glimpse of her vibrant red hair, a long wavy curl having loosened from her bonnet. She straightens at our approach, her posture confident as she rests her palm on the top of her shovel.

I don't recognize her from this distance. Do we have a new neighbor? I'm stirred from my thoughts by the sound of the others dismounting and tying their horses under the trees. I quickly do the same. The task complete, I lead the group toward the area where we were digging the roll. This new woman's bright blue eyes seem to follow me wherever I go, and I know not why.

"I see you've acquired a new friend," John says to his sister.

"I have," Charlie replies. "May I introduce Miss Hattie Miller."

Hattie Miller…. I can think of no Millers with daughters who live nearby.

Miss Miller moves her free hand forward but stops herself, pulling it back with an inhale. "Hello," she says with a melodic voice, a warm smile rising on her lips that meets her eyes.

Who is this woman, and where, exactly, did she come from? Why is she here helping fill the holes near my cabin? Her manner of greeting is so strange.

John speaks again. "I am Charlotte's brother, John, and this is my friend, Eric Thomas, who owns the cottage."

"Hi, John," Hattie says before meeting my eye directly. "Hello, Eric." I'm unsure whether it's my imagination, but she seems to have a strange lilt to her voice when she says my name.

"Good day," I manage to say with a nod. There's something unusual about her, though I can't quite place what it is.

John introduces her to the others as I survey the work that's been done in my absence. "My sister should not have enjoined you in her labors," John insists, speaking to the newcomer.

Embarrassment rushes over me when I realize I should have been the first to object to it. "Agreed," I tell her. "There's no need for you to be toiling with a shovel in my yard.

Her lips turn up in a reassuring smile. "It's all right. I like working outdoors."

I'm unable to place her unusual accent and her strange choice in words. "Where are you from, Hattie?" I ask.

She opens her mouth to reply but no words come out.

"She's from Seattle," Charlie says quickly.

I tilt my head to the side, knitting my brow. "I am unfamiliar with such a place. Is it to the north?"

Charlie interrupts loudly before Hattie can answer. "We need to get back to this hole. It's only half finished."

"Yes, we do," Hattie agrees. "It's nice to meet you, Eric… everyone." She has a pleasant smile and seems to genuinely mean that. She goes back to work, and I watch for a few moments, wondering at a woman as lovely as her volunteering to work alongside youngsters in the yard. I wish to inquire more of this unusual woman. I hope for an appropriate moment to speak with her later.

"In which of these holes are we to dig?" Nathaniel's inquiry pulls me from my thoughts.

"To the left there," I explain, gesturing toward our latest dig which finally struck water. Turning, I meet John's gaze. He narrows his eyes slightly and raises a brow just as faintly. My friend knows me well, and has likely noticed my prolonged attention to Miss Miller. I shrug and let it go. Who wouldn't be curious about a strange woman showing up on his property to perform manual labor? I turn to secure my shovel.

"Let's get to it, lads," John says, moving toward the spot where we hit water earlier.

The physical work is a welcome reprieve from my thoughts. I know nothing about this woman outside the few words we have just exchanged. Yet, I cannot help but wonder where she materialized from. John doesn't know her, so she can't be a long-time friend of his sister's. I glance over at her as I dig. She tucks that wayward strand of hair back into her bonnet and meets my eye with an expression I cannot read before she goes back to digging.

For some reason, I feel like I should know who she is—and she's looking at me as if we've met before. But I cannot place her.

We reach a point in the well that will fit only two men to continue the work. The Robinson brothers volunteer to dig for this portion while Richard and Isaac shovel away the dirt they excavate. This allows me, John, and my brothers to visit my supply of sandstone and cart over rocks to secure the well's walls.

"She's quite lovely," John whispers when my brothers are some distance ahead.

"Who?"

The corner of his mouth curls up into a smirk. "I am quite certain you know exactly who I speak of."

"Oh, the Miller girl? I hadn't really noticed." That is, of course, not the truth, but John need not know that. It is impossible to miss the fact that she is a lovely woman, but that is neither here nor there.

John only laughs and shrugs his shoulders, leaving me to ponder what he's getting at.

I consider his observation. I did experience an unusual reaction when I met Hattie, and I am intrigued by this woman. Her kindness at insisting on helping with the well is admirable. She carries herself with poise and confidence, and her smile is quite pleasant.

Yet, the threat of war still troubles my soul. "We need not be discussing such matters now, John. I have no doubt we'll be called to another battle soon," I tell him. "It is not the time to consider seeking courtship."

"Our lives are ever changing," he counters. "It may never be the right time. Yet, we must grasp those moments as they come to us."

I nod and softly exhale. "Wise words as always, my friend," I say. "But I know nothing about this woman."

"There is only one way to find out." He gives a wink and chuckles as we catch up to my brothers who have already begun loading the stones. We step in to assist, and the labor is a welcome distraction from John's comments.

When we return with the load, Charlie trudges over to me with Hattie by her side. Miss Miller stands closer to me than she did before. She is a lovely woman, with bright eyes and a smattering of freckles across the bridge of her nose and cheeks.

"Do you have another task we can assist with?" Charlie asks.

I pull my eyes away from the stranger, the urge to repeat my question about where she comes from dying on my lips. "No, thank you, Charlie. Not at the moment."

Charlie lifts her shoulders in an exaggerated shrug. "Come, Hattie.

I'll show you some more of the grounds, and my parents are anxious to meet you."

But instead of turning to follow her, Hattie turns to me and reaches for my arm, squeezing it and pulling it toward her. I inhale sharply with surprise. I've never had a young woman touch me so freely before. I find myself leaning toward her, wondering what it is she has gone to such lengths to gain my attention about. "Please, Mr. Thomas," she says, her eyes meeting mine with desperate intensity. "Would you consider putting a ladder inside of your well?"

"A ladder?" I am, once again, confused by her. "Whatever for?"

She purses her lips together and shifts on her feet, releasing my arm as if she just realized she'd been holding it. With a shrug, she says, "It's a deep well. There are a lot of children here that may be playing nearby. What if, God forbid, one of them falls in? Wouldn't it be a good idea for them to be able to climb back out?"

It takes a moment for her suggestion to settle into me, her sudden inquiry taking me by surprise. Yet the idea is interesting, and I gaze into her eyes that display a hint of some mysterious knowledge I cannot grasp.

My head rocks with affirmation, and I call out to the men around me. "We will be sure to include a ladder in this well's construction as a measure of safety."

"Very well." John steps up next to me. "Perhaps we can fashion it by means of placing the rocks so that should anyone fall in, they can climb out. We wouldn't want the wood to rot."

"That's a great idea. Thank you," Hattie says softly. She turns to leave. I feel the cool breeze between us and wish she were not walking away. I still haven't gotten the answer to any of my questions. Who is she, and why does she look at me like she knows a secret? An ache of regret fills my gut. Why had I not offered another chore that might keep her here longer?

"Eric?"

I whip my head around to face Colin, and he chuckles. "Brother, I called your name three times. Whatever is it that has your mind distracted?"

"I am just considering the placement of well rocks," I insist. "Why did you call me?"

"I was inquiring about how many more stones you believe we require," he replies.

I consider those we've brought versus the depth of the well. "I believe we will need at least three more loads," I tell him.

John eyes me with agreement. "We should hurry," he tells the others. "We've much to do to have a well dug and framed before sunset."

"Aye," Colin says, stepping away toward the stone pile.

John turns back to me. "I have a design in mind for the means of exiting the well, should anyone fall in," he says, his expression quite serious, which helps pull my thoughts away from all distractions. "I suggest we build it so rocks protrude at even distances, with others placed such that one could grasp hold."

"A fine idea." I manage to set aside thoughts of Miss Miller, and join him by the stones, where we stack those whose shapes may suit this plan.

"We're ready to begin setting stones," Nathaniel calls from inside the well, so I head over. "Any deeper and its integrity will falter."

"Fine work," I tell him. "Levi, get the rope. Let's get our friends out, and John and I will take their place to secure the stones." It takes a strong heave from the rest of us to pull the men out. Once they're on solid ground, John and I get to work.

The hard labor continues as the day draws on, and each time I set a stone that forms the exit, Miss Miller enters my thoughts. The questions I wish to ask her run through my mind. For example, she said she's from Seattle, but I know of no such place. How did she get here, and how does Charlie know her?

Hours later, clean, cool water pools up, settling against the strong stone walls. The men let out a raucous cheer. I join them, glad to see I am one step closer to completing my home. "Well done, lads," I tell the men, and we move toward the shade of the nearby trees save for Levi, who lowers the rope to bring up a fresh bucket of cool water.

John takes a sip from the scoop Levi passes around. "A fine taste it has," he declares.

He holds it out to me, and I close my eyes to enjoy the cold, crisp water. It has been a long day, but one full of triumph. With the help of my friends, I've gotten one step closer to finishing the house I've dreamed of for so many years.

I am truly blessed to have such wonderful brothers and such amazing friends. I truly appreciate their help.

And the help of a stranger, thoughts of which I simply cannot break free of.

CHAPTER NINE

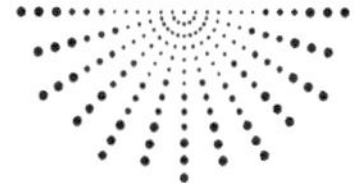

I KEEP PACE BESIDE CHARLIE AS WE HEAD TOWARD HER HOUSE. IT WAS... unsettling, meeting Eric Thomas. I hardly knew what to say to him. The man who built the lovely stone cottage was standing right in front of me, two and a half centuries before I first admired his work. I have so many questions for him. It would have been amazing to stay there and watch him build the well. I wish I'd had more time to talk to him.

Was he the ghost I saw in the woods that night?

He's incredibly good-looking, and that took me by surprise. In fact, he's the most attractive man I'd ever seen. It was hard not to stare at his handsome face, tan and symmetrical with a powerful jawline. Or that raven-black hair. His brown eyes reveal strength and determination. They're the eyes of a man who carefully crafted such a perfect little cottage in the woods. And the man whose strong sense of duty will take him to the front lines of a dangerous war.

Inhaling sharply at the thought, my heart stings as if a dagger has just stabbed through it. Eric is going to die in the war... in just a few short days. Why does someone like him have to lose his life, right at the point when he's just building one for himself?

"Hattie, are you well?"

I turn to Charlie, realizing I've stopped right in the middle of the forest path. "I-I'm all right." How could I possibly tell her that Eric is going to die?

She takes my right hand and cradles it between both hers. "Goodness, Hattie," she says. "Your hands are shaking as if you've spied a ghost." Her eyes soften as she looks into mine. "Perhaps you are still feeling the effects of the head injury. Would you like to sit, or perhaps go to my room to lie down?"

"No, I'll be fine," I tell her, though chills rush over me. I know Eric will die in the battle, but how many of the men I just spoke to will lose their lives in a few days as well? I don't want to upset Charlie, so I force a smile. "I'd love to see more of your home."

She narrows her eyes slightly as though she's not quite convinced. But she nods, patting my hand before letting it go. "Very well. But please do tell me if you're not feeling well."

"I will, I promise." I inhale deeply, letting out a slow cleansing breath as we continue toward the house. I'm having a hard time wrapping my mind around all of this. Is it possible I could make a difference here somehow?

Why am I even here?

We step inside the house, and I let Charlie lead me through the hallway, eerily reminded of how Nina and I had explored it just the night before.

"Here's the drawing room," Charlie announces. "This is one of my favorites. It's a lovely place to relax."

I feel a light chill on the back of my neck as I enter the room. It's so familiar, yet everything in it is brand new. The air is crisp and fresh, without any candles covering the scent of age. The wedding portrait above the fireplace is more vibrant than I remember, cleared of some yellowing I hadn't even noticed before. I recall the questions I had about the unrecognizable hint of emotion in the woman's eyes.

Perhaps all my questions will be answered now that I'm here.

WEARING FRESH DRESSES, CHARLIE AND I MAKE OUR WAY DOWN TO THE dining room. We've toured the whole house all afternoon, so I don't need to hide my familiarity with the place as we step in. The only chairs occupied at the immense oak table are those of Charlie's parents, who are seated at either end.

I instantly recognize the woman in the portrait, though now aged a couple of decades, as she turns when we enter.

"Father, Mother, I'd like to introduce Miss Hattie Miller," Charlie says before stepping aside.

Both of them stand, and Charlie's mother reaches me first. "Miss Miller, we're so pleased to meet you." She smiles as she offers a welcoming hand. I take it, admiring her warm-toned auburn hair that's just a shade darker than Charlie's. She looks youthful, especially for a mother of six, with only a hint of crow's feet at her temples. "I'm Frances Monroe, and this is my husband, Henry. We're delighted you'll be staying with us."

"I'm glad to meet you, too, Mr. and Mrs. Monroe," I reply. "It's so kind of you to let me stay here."

I know my accent probably sounds strange to them, as well as some of the words I choose, but there's not a trace of hesitation in Mrs. Monroe's eyes. "Please, call me Frances," she says kindly. "And we're happy to have you here. Now, more than ever, people must stick together." I can see the powerful emotion in her eyes. Is it what I saw in the portrait? But now it's clear, a mix of fear, uncertainty… and also, hope.

"Thank you, Frances." I turn my gaze toward Henry. He appears much older than his wife thanks to his balding crown, and perhaps the heavily burdened look in his eyes. The tufts of hair that do remain are strawberry blond. His skin is much paler than John's, hinting at little time spent outdoors recently.

"It is a pleasure to meet you, Miss Miller." His tone is gentle, warm and friendly. He gives me a welcoming nod.

"The pleasure is mine," I tell him.

"Hattie is such a lovely name." Frances gestures toward a chair near her end of the table. "Please, have a seat. We've set a place for you next to Charlie."

"Thank you," I tell her. "I hope you didn't go to too much trouble."

"None at all," Henry answers, holding out my chair and helping me scoot it in before doing the same for his wife. They share a loving glance, their hands touching lightly before he returns to his end of the table.

Frances turns to me as Charlie takes her seat, opening her mouth to say something. But she's interrupted as the four younger children stride into the room, chattering among themselves. They quickly quiet down and take their seats when their father gives them a firm glance.

"Have you met the children?" Frances asks.

"I have." I look around the table, pointing to each one as I identify them. "Matthew, Clayton, Elizabeth, and Penelope were out at the cottage with us." Penelope looks away when I say her name, but not before I see her smile.

"Charlie, perhaps Miss Miller would have preferred exploring the library to watching the men build," Frances suggests.

"I truly enjoyed watching the cottage construction," I insist, leaving off the part about shoveling dirt. "And the library is fascinating as well. I'd love to spend more time there." When Charlie took me there earlier, I realized little had changed over the centuries. Of course, Uncle Arthur's scrapbook was missing, as well as a few sets of shelves that must have been added later.

"You enjoy reading?" Frances asks.

"Very much so," I reply. "I'm a teacher… back home."

Frances smiles. "Well, that's lovely. Do you teach at a dame school?"

But before I can answer, Clayton chimes in, a bright red curl dangling over his eye.

"John helps us with our arithmetic after lessons," he says. "Even the girls."

"Our eldest son enjoys helping with the children's education,"

Frances explains. She turns to her son. "Clayton, is your brother coming in for supper?"

"He said soon," Elizabeth answers for him.

"Very good," Henry says. He turns to me. "Please feel free to explore the library collection anytime," Henry says. "When you stay with the Monroes, you are family."

A flush of warmth surges through me. *If only he knew.*

John arrives shortly after, slightly winded. "I apologize for my tardiness," he says. "We only recently finished the well." He nods politely at me.

"It seems you're making good progress," Henry says.

"We are," John says. "I'll be ready to start on the stable repairs shortly."

"Very well. Would you say grace tonight?" Henry asks.

I bow my head with the rest of the family, and John leads the prayer. It's clear that he holds an important place in this family, caring for his siblings, his parents, and their property. I wonder whether he will be present when Eric is killed in battle. It's likely since they're such good friends. It'll surely devastate him.

An ominous feeling clouds my heart at the thought.

Late that night, I lay across from Charlie in the other bed. "So, unfortunately, the British did capture the redoubt eventually," I tell her.

She gazes at me, her eyes wide in the moonlight, balanced on her elbows near the edge of her bed as I explain the Battle of Bunker Hill. I'd struggled to decide how much to tell her. I was sure when I hid the map that I'd try to help the colonists win. But I hadn't thought through all the repercussions. Anything that is changed by my being here could alter the future—for better or worse—forever.

But I didn't think it would do any harm telling Charlie about it. Men fought wars in this century, and I doubt they'd listen to a seventeen-year-old girl telling them they need a different strategy. Still, there's one part I do decide to keep to myself—Eric's impending death, and the fact that his cottage will sit empty for two and a half centuries afterward.

I'll save that for another day, if I tell her at all.

"If the British win this battle, what hope do we have for victory?" she asks in a whisper.

"The battle shows the colonists they are stronger than they thought," I explain. "They kill more soldiers than the British , and it empowers them to come together and fight harder. In the end, the colonists lose this battle, but it inspires them to win the war."

She squirms closer to the edge of the bed, her eyes gleaming with excitement. "What happens next?" she asks.

"Well, there are some struggles before they are able to develop a stable government." I swing my legs over the bed and sit up straight. "But eventually, they ratify the Constitution of the United States, and George Washington becomes the first president."

"General Washington?"

"Yes, that's right."

She scoots around to bring her own legs over the end of her bed, sitting right across from me. She crinkles her forehead, drawing her lips into a frown. "But that's just one man in charge again—a king. How is that different?"

"Believe me, it's much different," I tell her. "The Constitution's framework keeps him from having too much power by himself. Everything the men are fighting for here is going to change the world."

"Then I shall be honored to be a part of it," she says, her eyes determined.

I give her a nod. "That's right. Any support you can give means you are part of this incredible moment in history."

She bites her bottom lip, considering this for a moment before whispering, "I'll be part of history."

I'm not exactly sure what she means by that, but I'm too tired to think about it right now. "It's getting late. We should get some sleep."

"Goodnight, Hattie." She crawls back into her bed and under the covers.

I try to lay back and relax. How will I even fall asleep after everything I've experienced today? Traveling back in time, meeting the man who built the cottage, and my Monroe ancestors—a part of me wishes this is all just a dream. If it is, I hope I will wake up soon to find Nina in the bed next to mine.

But this is all too real. I know I'm not dreaming.

I stare at the ceiling long after Charlie drifts off, her breath falling into a steady, even pattern. What is my family thinking right now? Do they miss me? Do they even know I'm gone?

If they do, I'm sure they're in a panic. How will they know I'm all right, just not there with them in the future?

And how will I ever get home?

CHAPTER TEN

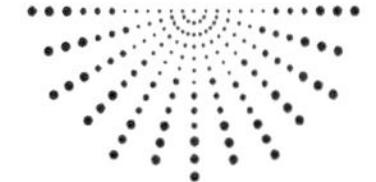

HATTIE

"IT'S FORTUNATE WE ARE CLOSE TO THE SAME SIZE," CHARLIE MURMURS as she helps lace up my corset. "It's too bad we do not have a dress-maker scheduled to visit any time soon. Perhaps after the war ends."

The thought of staying long enough to need to have my own clothes made causes a knot to form in my stomach. It's been surreal to meet everyone and see what life was like in the 1700s, but I want to go home. I can only imagine how scared my family must be that they can't find me anywhere.

After getting me into all of the underclothes required, she pulls a dress out of the wardrobe. "This is one of my favorite church dresses," she explains. "I'd like you to wear it."

"Are you sure?" I can see why she likes it. The full floral skirt is lovely, accented by a light blue jacket that matches the shade of the flowers exactly.

She takes it off the hanger. "I insist," she says. "You'll look beautiful in it."

"Thank you," I tell her.

She nods and helps me step into it.

For some reason, Eric has been on my mind since I woke up. He's handsome, that's for sure, so I find myself wanting to look my best if I run into him today. It seems ridiculous to want to flirt with a guy I know is about to die–one that I have no hope of a future with if I get to go home. Nevertheless, I keep seeing his face in my mind's eye. That strong jawline, inquisitive eyes, and perfectly straight nose. I haven't asked Charlie if he'll be at church, but I suspect he will. My breath catches in my throat as I think about it.

"Are you girls ready?" Frances calls up the stairs.

"Coming, Mother!" Charlie cups a hand around her mouth and yells far louder than necessary. They might have heard her in 2025.

Little jolts of electric flutters fill me as we head downstairs to get into the carriage. The possibility of seeing Eric begins to consume my every thought, despite my own warnings not to get involved. A girl has to have something to look forward to, especially if I might have to stay in this war torn period forever.

WE REACH THE CHURCH, AN IMPRESSIVE BUILDING WITH A POLISHED white spire jutting toward the sky, and I stop to admire it. I know it still exists in 2025, having passed it on the way to Great Aunt Ida's house. I'm anxious to look inside and experience a real church service of the 1700s.

John helps us ladies step out of the carriage. I look around, but there's no sign of Eric or any of the Thomases among the crowd. Frances and Charlie urge the Monroe children toward the brick church entrance, so I assist them.

I hitch a breath when we enter the sanctuary. Every detail, from hand-carved railings to stained glass windows, is elaborate. Its ceilings tower high above the congregation, with galleries on either side overlooking the mahogany pews below. Colorful beams of light shine through an enormous round, stained-glass window above the pulpit.

Its design depicts the nativity, with a surrounding landscape scene in breathtaking detail.

It takes me a moment to realize the family is separating, with the men going to the right. My forehead furrows in confusion. Why aren't we sitting together?

"This way," Charlie says, urging me forward. We step around the tall, intricately carved pew ends and sit toward the middle of the pew, fairly close to the front.

Once seated, I notice those ends obscure my view of the men, clearly by design. I try not to let out a sigh. There goes my opportunity to look for Eric. These people take their religious ceremonies seriously, that's for sure.

It's difficult to pay attention to the sermon. Not only does the preacher speak in a thick accent, using words I don't always understand, he's not that loud. I'm used to preachers using microphones. I do my best to pay attention, but it's difficult. I do stand and join in the hymns. A few of them I recognize. Others are so foreign, I may as well be singing in another language.

After the service, we reunite with the Monroe men and step outside the church. I stay next to Charlie and Frances, who introduce me to several ladies as we linger on the steps. I do my best to be polite, but I can't keep track of all of their names, and I'm hoping it doesn't matter anyway. I would really like to go home before the next service.

A familiar voice hits my ears, and that tension I've been feeling in my core flares up again. I suck in a deep breath and turn to look over my shoulder.

There he is. Eric Thomas. He's deep in conversation with a group of men, some of which I recognize from the day before. He's wearing a long black coat and breeches with a wide-brimmed hat, his expression somber. I bite my bottom lip, hoping he's okay. But then, he's probably talking about the war, the one that he's about to die in, so no, he's not okay.

"It's time for the church dinner," Charlie explains, looping her arm through mine. We follow the rest of the Monroes toward a large field behind the church. The grass is green and ripples in the slight breeze. I had no idea we were having a church dinner, but it seems like fun.

And maybe a chance to speak to Eric again.

The younger brothers run off to play with friends, and John and Henry appear with a picnic basket I hadn't seen them pack. Laughing and chattering, they walk over to join their group of friends, which, of course, includes Eric.

When I realize I'm staring, I quickly turn my attention to Charlie. I've just opened my mouth to ask her something when she runs off toward a group of boys. I watch as they prepare to play a game. It looks familiar, but I'm not sure what it is.

"We allow Charlie to participate." Francis leans down, keeping her voice soft. "We discovered long ago she is much happier when she has such freedoms."

"I totally get it," I tell her. "She's such a tomboy. I love it. She's a great kid."

Frances's face lights up with a mother's pride. "Thank you," she says a bit slower than expected. I wonder if she didn't understand every word that came out of my mouth the same way I struggled to understand the sermon. I need to be more aware of how I'm speaking.

I help Francis spread the picnic blanket before turning back to watch Charlie and her friends. They've been divided into teams, each with sticks and balls they hit along the ground. It looks a little bit like croquet, but I've never played that before, so I'm not certain. Whatever they're doing, Charlie seems to be holding her own. I have to giggle when she raises her hands in victory after tapping a ball into a pail. Some of the boys look less than amused.

"Would you excuse me, Hattie?" Frances asks. I turn back to her as she continues. "I need to get the younger girls settled in their activities."

"Can I help?" I offer.

She shakes her head. "No, that's not necessary, dear. I'll just be a few minutes. Please, relax here and enjoy the cool breeze."

"I will, thank you." I watch as she steps away with the girls and helps another mother lay out items on a large blanket. The girls giggle with excitement over what must be a craft to work on.

I close my eyes for a moment, taking in the laughter of the children playing all around me. This could be any normal Sunday in any century. But just miles away, bullets will start flying in just a few days. How many of these kids will lose a father, a brother, an uncle, a cousin?

"It's a lovely day."

My eyes fly open, and I'm staring into deep, chocolate brown ones. I inhale sharply before managing to say, "That it is."

"I wanted to thank you for your assistance with the well." His smile is kind, maybe a bit curious.

"It was nothing," I insist, waving a hand.

"On the contrary, it was quite helpful, and I appreciate it." He cocks his head slightly. "I've been wondering. What brings you to Boston?"

"My father was killed at the battle near the towns of Lexington and Concord," I explain, keeping up the story Charlie and I had agreed on. I inject some sadness into my voice, which isn't difficult at the moment. Just thinking about my family makes me tear up. "I have no other family. I hoped to find an acquaintance of his that lives nearby, or so I thought, but I bumped into Charlie, and she was so kind. The Monroes have all been so welcoming."

"My condolences about your father," he says. "That must've been very difficult for you. The Monroes are lovely, though. That was a bit of serendipity, I believe, that you found Charlie."

"They're wonderful people." I decide I'd better change the subject. "Your cottage is beautiful. It's so detailed. I particularly like the porches."

"It's kind of you to notice." His eyes light up a bit.

"How long have you been working on it?" I'm trying to think of questions he'll be happy to answer to keep him here a bit longer. It's not as if I can just blurt out that he's supposed to die at Bunker Hill. Besides, looking into those chocolate wells, watching his face light up when he's excited… I could get used to that.

"It has been two years since I laid the first stone," he explains. "Winter weather impeded the progress both years."

I nod. "I suppose the mortar wouldn't harden well in the cold."

He raises a brow. "That is correct. You are familiar with building with stone?"

"I-I watched my father build… when I was younger." It's a lie, of course. I just happened to assume that would be the case. Lucky guess.

"Then you have a bit of Charlie's spirit in you," he suggests.

I chuckle, shooting a quick gaze at Charlie as she taps in another ball. "Maybe a little bit." His eyes brighten as he laughs with me, and for a moment, that heavy weight of war seems to disappear from his countenance. I feel some of the stress leaving my shoulders as well.

"Charlie is quite… unique," he says. "And I can see now that you are as well."

I arch an eyebrow, not sure what to think about that.

He quickly amends, "In a good way, I assure you."

"Thank you." I smile demurely, looking up at him through my eyelashes.

He chuckles, looks away, and then meets my gaze again. "I believe I should join my family. It was lovely to see you again, Miss Miller."

"You as well, Mr. Thomas." I don't want him to leave. I have so much more I want to ask him, but I understand we can't stand here chatting forever. "Please give your family my regards."

Nodding, he takes a step away before pausing and saying, "I hope we can chat again soon."

I nod a bit more enthusiastically than I probably should. "Yes, I would like that."

He backs up a few steps before turning to walk away. I follow him with my gaze as he returns to his family and begins to talk to an older man who must be his father. The two of them look a lot alike. The older man is definitely what my sister would call a "silver fox."

I can't keep pretending that I'm only interested in Eric's cottage. He is intriguing to me, and it has nothing to do with my desire to keep him from dying.

I remember the map hidden in the alabaster box in Charlie's room. Maybe Uncle Arthur's ideas can turn the tide of the upcoming battle.

Maybe I can't save everyone… but maybe I can save Eric.

Settling into bed that night, Charlie props herself up on one elbow, facing me. "Tell me something about the future," she whispers. "What's it like for women there since you can wear trousers?"

"It's more than the clothes," I say quietly, turning and propping myself up the same way. "Most women have careers. We work and make our own money. We can buy our own houses if we want to."

"You don't say? That's amazing. What about wars? Can women fight?" She leans in a bit, mesmerized by my words.

I nod. "Yes, they can."

Her mouth falls open for a moment. She promptly closes it before whispering, "I should like to join the men in battle."

A rush of panic washes over me, but I resist the urge to tell her she's insane. It took a lot of courage for her to admit that to me. I don't want to be the one who keeps her from living the life she chooses, though I don't want her hurt or killed. "Please be careful, whatever you do," I tell her.

"I know the danger I face, and I will take care," she says, her expression determined. "But if my brothers can risk their safety to fight, so can I."

"You can, but I still care about you." The thought of leaving Charlie, or having her leave me by getting herself killed, has me tearing up a little. "I'm glad I came here because I got to meet you."

"I'm glad for it, too, Hattie," she replies. We're quiet for a moment before she leans in even closer. "I saw you speaking with Eric today. I haven't seen either of you smile so wide before."

I've already told Charlie so much, I may as well tell her everything. "Honestly, I think I'm starting to become… interested in him," I admit.

Even in the dim light, I notice her face brighten. "I was hoping as much."

"But I don't think I should feel that way since he's... since I don't know how long I'll be here." Now's not the time to tell her Eric is going to die. I couldn't speak the words if I had to.

She shakes her head briskly. "That does not matter. Feelings are not something you can willingly withhold. It is why I must play games with the boys and help with the cottage. I cannot deny what is a part of me."

"You have a point."

"I saw the look in his eyes," she adds. "I believe he does want to court you. Suppose he should ask you. How would you respond?"

I lay back on the pillow, looking up at the ceiling. "I honestly don't know how he feels about me, Charlie. I think I would like to get to know him better."

She flops down onto her back.. "What's it like, courtship in the future? How do you let a man know he should approach you?"

"Well, we approach them if we're interested."

She lets out an audible gasp. "Women do?"

"Yes, we don't need to wait for men to come to us," I explain.

"Fascinating. But what happens if the man you approach does not share your feelings?"

"Then we find out sooner rather than later," I tell her. "Rejection can be hard. But I guess if men have to deal with that, so should women."

"I suppose sometimes the risk is worth it," she says.

"Sometimes it is," I agree. "But telling Eric I'm beginning to have feelings for him would be a huge risk because I might pop back into the future anytime. If he does feel the same way about me, I wouldn't want to just disappear on him one day."

"I think you should tell him your feelings regardless," she says. She's quiet for a moment before whispering, "I think courtship in the future sounds much more interesting and adventurous."

"I suppose it is."

Even if I'm trapped here forever, I still may not have a chance with

Eric. Not if he's going to die soon. I can't stand the thought of losing him that way.

For a moment, I ponder the idea that he might actually be the reason I'm here. What if I'm meant to save his life?

Maybe it's why I'm on this grand adventure.

If so… that just might make it worth it.

CHAPTER ELEVEN

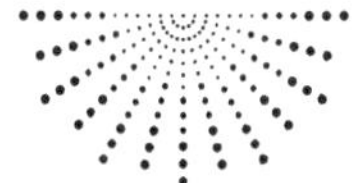

Hattie

After lunch the next day, I do my best to keep up with Charlie as she does chores around the property. I'm trying to help, but right now, all I can do is watch in awe as she shoes one of the horses. With each meticulous step of the process, her expression remains calm and thoughtful.

"You do that well," I tell her.

She looks up briefly before turning her gaze back to her work. "I've been doing it for many years, since I was eight or so, with help, of course."

"Eight?" I don't remember what I was doing at that age, but I know it wasn't handling a thousand pound animal.

"With some assistance, yes," she replies.

She continues hammering the shoe on as I watch. It's no wonder these people crave their independence. That fighting spirit is built into their DNA. It makes me reconsider the knowledge I've been withholding. Should I tell her about Eric's fate in the battle a few days away? I've gone back and forth on it a million times. If I do, maybe if we put our heads together, we can come up with a way to keep him safe. But then again, maybe she'll decide to put herself in harm's way, and the Monroe and Thomas families will mourn her instead of Eric.

And I still want to go home. Maybe now that the well is complete, I should just jump in and see if it gets me there. But if it does, I'll never see Eric again, and I'll never get a chance to really get to know him. I'd miss Charlie and her family—my family—terribly.

Once done, she secures the horse in its stall and looks at me. "I'm finished until tomorrow," she says. "We can do something fun now."

"What do you do for fun?" I ask.

"Would you like to go swimming?" The mischievous grin on her face nearly has me giggling.

"That sounds amazing," I say instead. "It's so hot today." I pause for a moment and consider the logistics of swimming in my long gown. "What will we wear?"

She grins at me, her eyes bright and playful. "You'll see. Follow me."

She takes me straight from the stables to the back of the property and into the woods. I didn't have time to explore this part in 2025, though Mom had talked about a small creek in the forest. But the rushing water in front of me is hardly a small creek. It's several feet deep and flows into a small pool that collects under a canopy of trees.

"This is beautiful," I tell her.

She nods enthusiastically. "This is my favorite place to swim," she explains, slipping out of her dress, folding it, and setting it on the grass. I follow her lead, and soon, we have everything off except our shifts. She runs for the water, splashing in a few feet before jumping up and diving under.

I need no convincing, following her and wading in until it's deep enough to dive under. Resurfacing, a refreshing chill rushes over me, and I flip my wet hair back, lifting my eyes to the canopy above. I lean back to float on my back, watching the leaves rustle on the branches above me while Charlie splashes around on the other side of the creek.

"It's too hot," a young male voice complains from somewhere behind the trees.

Charlie freezes, whispering, "Did you hear that?"

I glide toward the shore where I can get my footing, "I did." I whisper.

"Someone approaches," she says. "Hurry."

We jump out of the creek and run around to our piles of clothes by the trees. There's no time to lace up corsets, so we throw on our dresses over our wet shifts. She tosses the corsets and petticoats behind the nearest bush, just in time to see Eric and two young boys step through the trees.

"Oh, it's only you," Charlie says to the group, shaking her head. In an instant, she slips off her dress again and jumps into the water.

But I feel frozen in place by those now-familiar flutters in my stomach.

"Good afternoon, Miss Miller," Eric says. He keeps his eyes on mine without a glance at my wet dress. "It seems we all had the same idea."

"Can we go in?" one of the boys begs him.

Eric turns to him, breaking our gaze. "Yes, after you've said hello to the Monroes' guest, Miss Miller."

"Hello, Miss Miller," the young boys say in unison, already out of most of their clothes before they even finish saying my name.

"Hello, boys," I greet them.

"Please excuse my brothers," Eric says, and I turn back to him. "I'm afraid they cannot resist cool water on a hot summer day."

"It's all right," I assure him, my voice an octave higher than I intend. "What are their names?"

"The dark-haired one is Willie," he explains. "He's eight, and quite rude, I'm finding." His lips rise in a slight grin, and I'm glad to finally see that relaxed look in his deep brown eyes. "The blond-haired one is Luke," he adds. "He's six, so he has an excuse."

"I suppose the world is full of wonder at six," I tell him. "I can't blame either of them for wanting to be in the water. It's very refreshing."

"Please, don't let me keep you from enjoying it," he says.

I feel a twinge of heat rising in my cheeks. I can't take my dress off with him standing here, even though my shift is far more clothes than I'd usually wear swimming. "It's all right. I just needed a quick dip to cool off."

He nods softly, turning his eyes to the boys in the water.

"One, two… three!" Charlie's countdown draws my attention as well, and I watch as the boys race each other across the pond.

"Charlie is quite easy to love, isn't she?" I ask.

Eric nods, his eyes focused on the contest. "She is."

"I have a feeling that's not the way everyone feels about her uniqueness."

"Sadly, no." He turns to me. "I'm afraid many of the ladies in town trouble Mrs. Monroe about 'controlling her daughter.' They insist it's unladylike to play games with boys."

"That's ridiculous," I insist. "Everyone has a right to be themselves, to be happy."

He turns to me. "I agree. And so do the Monroes."

Taking a seat on the shore, I turn back to the water, where Charlie and the boys have already started on another game that involves skipping rocks. Eric settles nearby. "She's at home with you and your brothers. It's as if you are an extension of her own family."

"Precisely," he says. "Our families have lived on this land since before we were born. I cannot recall ever actually meeting her brother John. He has simply been there, always."

"You two are very close."

"We are like brothers," he confirms.

We fall into a comfortable silence, just watching Charlie and the boys play in the water. Birds chatter in the trees above us. The scent of lilac reaches us with the gentle breeze that chills me lightly through my still-wet hair. I think of all the questions I had for Eric before I came here, when he was, to me, just a ghost of a man who built a charming cottage in the woods.

"Was it your parents who made their way to the colonies?" I ask after a while.

He shakes his head. "My father arrived when he was very young," he explains. "And my mother was born here, so it was my grandparents on both sides who made the journey."

"That's very brave of them."

"It was," he agrees. "Grandfather Thomas often told the stories of their passage across the ocean. My father was four years old at the time, and his sister was three. His mother was with child."

I can't even imagine crossing the ocean in those days, much less doing it pregnant and with young kids. "I would love to hear his stories," I tell him.

"Unfortunately, he passed years ago," he says sadly. "But I remember every story he ever told. I hope to tell them to my own children one day, in the house I've built."

My heart sinks at the thought of his death in the war, and I pause for a moment. "I'm sure your future family will love to hear them." Maybe I will save him, and he can have that future.

"I hope so," he says quietly.

"When did your parents—" I begin, but Charlie's voice cuts me off.

"Luke?" There's something in her voice I've never heard from her before, an uncertainty, bordering on panic. "Luke!" she repeats. This time it's a shriek, the kind that makes my blood run cold, a sound I'd heard too many times before from my lifeguard tower back home.

Eric and I step forward, scanning the water. Willie stands frozen near the bank closest to us.

I don't see Luke.

"What's happening?" Eric demands.

"Luke! Luke!" Charlie screams again, splashing in the water as if she could move it aside to look under it.

"I don't see him," I tell Eric, looking for the telltale signs of someone in trouble in the water, but all I see is Charlie's splashing.

"Neither do I." His eyes lock on the water, darkening with concern.

Eric and I sprint toward the creek. He gets there first, diving in without hesitation. A chill washes over me as the pool of water closes in behind him.

"Willie, come over here," I call out. Luckily, he listens to me and wades out of the water. I wrap my arm around his shivering body. He's clearly in shock.

I lock my eyes on the place where Eric jumped in and start counting down the seconds as my heart thumps wildly. Time draws out as the seconds turn into minutes.

He doesn't come up for air.

"Charlie, come here!" My call meets deaf ears. Wide eyed and panicked, she keeps screaming Luke's name, but at least she is standing in the shallow part. If she stays put, she shouldn't be in Eric's way.

I scan the water again and see a swirl where Eric must be underwater. He's approaching the time limit where even the best swimmers run out of breath, but he's not resurfacing.

He's risking his own life to save Luke.

A shiver creeps up my spine, and I realize this might be why Eric will die in battle—he will be protecting someone he cares about. Yes, he's willing to give his life for the colony's independence, but there's a deeper cause that drives him. He's not capable of turning his back on someone he loves for his own life or comfort. His older brothers will be there beside him, and his best friend John.

He's going to protect them all. My breath catches in my throat, and I hold Willie a little tighter.

I keep my eyes on the water. Unless Eric has trained for this, he won't be able to hold his breath much longer. I doubt he will come up without Luke.

Just as I'm thinking about jumping in, a wild splash shoots straight up as Eric surfaces, holding Luke in his arms. I exhale with relief until I see the boy's condition—limp and lifeless.

"Bring him here!" I shout, loosening my grip on Willie. "Stay right here," I tell the boy, and he nods, his eyes wide with fear.

Eric doesn't hesitate, not even to catch his own breath, swimming to the shore then running as soon as his feet can touch the creek bed.

"Lay him down." I nod toward a grassy area, and Eric sets his brother down quickly yet gently, with a look of desperation I haven't seen in him before. But as he gazes at his brother, darkness surfaces in his eyes. I realize none of them have heard of CPR in 1775.

He thinks his brother is dead and that nothing can help him.

"Move!" I tell him, trying to break through Eric's grief so I can start working on the boy. Eric has given everything in him to save his brother, and now, it's up to me.

I just pray it's not too late.

CHAPTER TWELVE

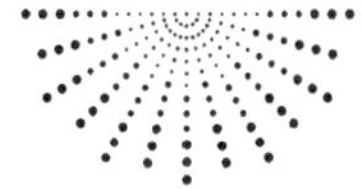

Eric

LUKE LIES MOTIONLESS ON THE GROUND IN FRONT OF ME. MY HEART thumps wildly against my ribcage. His limbs resemble those of a rag doll. I turn his head and gaze in horror at his pale face. Eyes are glazed, and his lips are frozen, darkening and turning deep blue.

The stillness is what unsettles me most. It is something I have seen far too many times before, those images burned into my mind. So many men on the battlefield, friend and enemy alike, left in this unmovable state of soullessness. And now I see it in my own young brother.

He's dead.

An ache the weight of a ball of lead forms in my chest. Air freezes in my lungs. Life has left my brother's body.

"Move!"

The command sounds hollow, distant.

I feel firm palms shoving against my chest. "Eric, get out of the way!"

Startled at the sound of my name, I look up. Hattie's eyes flash with authority, and I release Luke's arms, staring blankly at the imprints my fingers have left on them.

I rise, mindlessly stepping backward as Hattie kneels and examines him. Her fingers feel for a pulse I know does not exist.

Loud wails erupt next to Hattie, grabbing my attention. Willie stands there, wild tears pouring down his face. I reach an arm out to him, and he steps around Hattie and falls against me. Holding him tightly, I make no effort to silence his crying.

She continues to tend to Luke in a way that is foreign to me. She repositions him, holding his head up, his chin pointed toward the sky.

I hear splashing behind me as Charlie approaches, and I turn to look at her. Though she's drenched, I can still nearly discern which of the drops on her cheeks are tears.

"What is Hattie doing?" she asks.

All I can do is shake my head from side to side. "I do not know." I offer her my other arm, and the three of us stand transfixed while Hattie continues her… efforts.

"Is he—" Charlie does not finish her sentence.

"Yes." I can barely choke out the word. She covers her face with her palms, and I feel her body jerking with quiet sobs. The moments press on as we stare at the scene before us.

A dark cloud of horror descends upon my heart. I see our mother's face, already tight from the worry about her sons old enough to go off to war, only to receive this news of her youngest child. Her heart will shatter at losing him, and I fear she will never recover.

I imagine my father, a proud, good man, having been closely involved with the war effort. His spirit will now be flattened by this loss. Redcoats be damned, he may take up the rifle himself despite his age, leaving no enemy standing.

And I… I have yet to feel much beyond the heavy wound in my heart, Willie's shaking, wailing body beside me, and Charlie's cold, dripping hair and muffled sobs.

Hattie repositions herself, pinching Luke's nose shut.

"Now what is she doing?" Charlie whispers.

"I do not know," is all I can answer.

Hattie bends over, blowing air into Luke's blue, parted lips, and I don't understand why. She has tended to my brother's body too long. It is time to inform my parents and arrange for his burial. There is no reason to delay the inevitable.

"Hattie, I—" I begin.

But she cuts me off. "Trust me!" she shouts. "I know what I'm doing!"

I go silent, somehow feeling that trust build in me and—dare I admit it—the tiniest shimmer of hope. She blows into his mouth again, then positions her hands over his chest and begins pressing down in solid, rhythmic movements.

"You'll hurt him!" Charlie calls.

I open my mouth to tell her no one can hurt Luke anymore, that he is beyond pain. But hearing Willie's shaking sobs, I stifle my reaction.

"Just wait," Hattie says, her voice calm, determined. She silently counts the number of hand presses, then goes back to his mouth to blow into it again.

I watch her graceful, purposeful motions as she repeats the pattern again. Luke's tiny body jerks with each movement. Even I begin to fear for him, though I know the thought is irrational. Still, I let go of Willie and Charlie and step forward, moving my arm in to pull Hattie away from him.

"Hattie—" I begin, but my words catch in my throat.

Movement stirs from the ground below Hattie. My arm freezes mid-air as I realize it is Luke, moving of his own accord. My heart jumps, skipping a beat.

His gurgling sounds quickly turn into hacking coughs. Hattie rolls him onto his side, where he spits out mouthfuls of water between each choking gasp. She rubs his back and looks up to me with a bright, relieved smile.

I scarcely know how to react, my heart and nerves caught in a frenzy of emotion. Through the efforts of this woman, and a miracle of God, my brother lives!

I drop to the ground again while Hattie moves to the other side of

Luke. She continues to rub his back while I brush his drenched hair off his face and touch his warming cheek. He continues to cough, and Hattie slowly moves him up into a sitting position.

Silently, I wrap my arms around him, careful to give him room to breathe. He coughs in spasms against my chest, but it is the most beautiful sound I have ever heard.

After a few moments, I release him to allow Willie and Charlie to hold him, and I turn my gaze to Hattie. She sits on the grass by Luke, her knees pulled up to her chest as she steadies her breath. What miraculous procedure has she done to save my brother? She did it with such quick action, with self-assurance and expertise.

Luke coughs again, taking me out of my thoughts and drawing Hattie's attention as well. "We should get him inside," she says.

I squat next to Luke and meet his eye. "I'm going to carry you home." He nods softly, still coughing into his hand. I turn to Charlie. "I need you to fetch Dr. Langley."

Charlie nods, quickly slipping her dress over her head. Hattie is there in an instant helping her fasten the back. Charlie takes off running without another word, lifting her skirt almost to her knees to aid her speed. I return my attention to Luke, scooping him up and adjusting him so he'll be comfortable. Hattie already has Willie by the hand, following behind us as I quickly make my way through the woods.

Though I make haste, my mind wanders. The ache in my gut has subsided, fleeting away with Luke's every movement in my arms. He is well, warm, and his breath is steady, though occasionally interrupted by coughing. I was so certain of his death, that familiar darkness washing over me as it had at the sight of my fallen companions in battle. To my knowledge, no one has ever used such a procedure to restore breath. But Luke… his revival was so sudden, quivers of fear still echo through my veins. My heartbeat still pounds out of rhythm, and confusion still clouds my mind.

Hattie saved Luke's life.

We pass my cottage, but I continue on toward my family home, anxious to deliver a frightened—but alive—Luke to our mother's arms. Perhaps then, I will have the time to ask Hattie about her efforts.

The canopy of trees thins as we reach the main grounds of our property, and I pick up speed toward the house, glancing over my shoulder to be sure Hattie and Willie have kept pace. Hattie's hand is clasped protectively over his as they both run only a few yards behind me. She holds her skirt in her free hand.

Finally, we reach the back entrance. "Mother!" I call while I throw open the door with one hand, leaving it open for the others.

I hear her light footsteps on the stairs before Mother appears through the kitchen doorway, her eyes widening when she sees Luke in my arms. "What happened?" she demands, running toward us with arms outstretched.

I release Luke, who reaches for her. Mother falls to her knees to set him on the ground, moving his hair and clothes aside to examine him. "He went under in the creek," I explain quickly.

She gasps, her eyes meeting mine. "How long was he underwater?"

"About three minutes," Hattie answers for me.

Mother whips her head around to gaze at her. "Three minutes? How is this possible? How is he not—" She turns back to Luke, placing both her palms on his cheeks before pulling him into an embrace and kissing the top of his head. "My baby," she says softly.

"Miss Miller performed some sort of procedure," I try to explain.

"He should probably lie down until the doctor can look him over," Hattie suggests quickly, not elaborating on my statement.

I nod toward my mother. "Dr. Langley is on his way."

Mother pulls back from Luke, taking his face in her hands again. "Can you walk?" she asks him.

He nods weakly, and she stands, wrapping her arm around him. "We'll get him to the parlor. Abigail, please get him some warm broth."

"Yes, ma'am." I hadn't even noticed our cook entering the room.

I follow my mother and stand by the divan while she comforts Luke. Hattie follows, and I notice she hasn't dropped Willie's hand until now. He seems so calm considering the circumstances as he stands next to Mother. Gazing at the reassuring expression on Hattie's lovely face, I can see why. She has managed to save one of my brothers while comforting the other.

I am astounded by her. Truly.

After a few moments, I hear the click of hoof steps approach the still-open back door and go to escort the doctor inside. I quickly lead him to the parlor, with Charlie following. Mother stands and steps aside.

The doctor frowns. "I was told this boy drowned in the creek."

"He did," I confirm. "He was lifeless when I found him and managed to pull him out after a few minutes."

Dr. Langley knits his bushy brows so tightly they nearly touch. "How is it that he appears so well?"

It is not a question I can answer, but I attempt it. "Miss Miller completed a procedure that restored his breathing," I say, gesturing toward Hattie.

"Procedure?" the doctor asks, turning to her.

"I gave him CP—I performed chest compressions and forced breaths to expel the water from his lungs," Hattie explains. I watch as she demonstrates where she positioned her hands. The process seems simple, yet brilliant.

"I have never heard of such a procedure," the doctor says. "How did you come to know how to do this?"

All eyes, including mine, lock to Hattie, who inhales before answering. "I swam a lot as a child and learned about safety from those around me."

I furrow my brow, confused. The explanation makes sense, yet even our own doctor has no knowledge of the procedure for restoring breath. Perhaps there are new developments in Hattie's hometown that have yet to reach Boston.

The doctor places his ear against Luke's chest and examines his eyes, ears, and mouth. "He appears to be well," he announces. "Ensure he rests until at least tomorrow. If anything seems amiss, send for me again."

"I will, thank you," I tell him firmly.

He picks up his medical bag, taking one more look at Hattie before wishing my mother well and walking out the door.

I gaze at Hattie, mesmerized. So many questions circle through my mind as my eyes meet hers. A pleasant warmth rises in my chest, catching me by surprise. So much about her is a mystery, yet I have seen such extraordinary action from her. She is kind, accepting, and nurturing, yet she is fierce and confident when needed, as well as intelligent and capable.

How did she come to be here just when we needed her most?

Who is this remarkable girl?

CHAPTER THIRTEEN

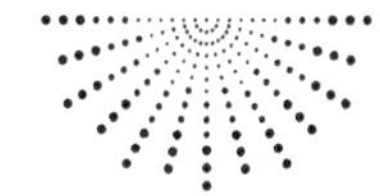

"It starts today." Those are the first words that come out of my mouth, my eyes still flickering open. The thought whisks away any sleepiness, my mind filling with dread.

Charlie is already out of bed, pulling open the curtains. I ponder how ironically cheerful her face looks in the orange rays of sunrise. How can the world seem so normal when everything is about to fall apart?

"The militia will send for the men soon, correct?" she asks.

I nod, pulling the covers away and swinging my legs off the bed. "It's Tuesday, June 13. Today, the colonial leaders will learn that the British are planning to fortify the hills around Boston. They'll decide to send militia to Bunker Hill." I'd read all the details in Aunt Ida's library books. Now, the words on those pages seem so cold and distant compared to the real fear growing in me. Eric is going out to the battlefield soon, along with his brothers and neighbors... and Charlie's brother.

But Eric won't return. A boulder forms in my stomach, and my heart thumps against my chest. I can't let him go....

"The men will leave as soon as they're alerted," she says, plopping down on the bed beside me. "Are you sure we will lose the battle?"

"Unfortunately, yes," I say sadly. "The British will win, although it will be a decisive battle for the country's success overall." I hesitate to tell her the rest but find myself saying it anyway. "Eric will be one of the many casualties."

A long moment of silence passes over us, and I fidget nervously with the stitching on my nightgown. Though my stomach clenches inside, I'm grateful to have Charlie as a friend and confidant. I don't know how I would have dealt with all of this alone.

"I think you should warn him," she says after a long, somber pause.

"Do you think he'll believe that I'm from the future?" I look at her hopefully.

She lifts her shoulders in a shrug. "Maybe you don't need to tell him that part. But he cannot go into battle unwarned."

I exhale slowly. "Okay. But that'll be hard with so many people around."

"Leave it to me," she says, her mouth tipping into a crooked grin. "After dinner, I'll arrange for a meeting for you and Eric tonight when it's dark. Such a thing is normally forbidden without a chaperone, but after all, you're not from here. You're from a much more exciting, wonderful future."

I pull her in for a hug, my heart racing. While I'm excited to have the opportunity to speak to Eric again, I'll have to find a way to convince him to be careful without making him think I'm insane.

It won't be easy.

SOFT MOONLIGHT ILLUMINATES THE FOREST PATH LEADING TO ERIC'S cottage. The ache in my stomach is still palpable, but the thrill of seeing him again has my pace quickening. The darkness around me makes my journey feel shadowy, forbidden, and a shiver passes over me.

My heart flutters uncontrollably when I see him sitting on the porch, an empty rocking chair beside him. He smiles and stands as I approach.

"Good evening, Miss Miller," he says.

"Good evening, Mr. Thomas." It seems strange to be so formal. But as Charlie has explained, it's considered impolite not to be so. I'm surprised he's agreed to meet me here, considering it's taboo for us to be alone together. Either Eric is uncomfortable with it, or he's worried that I am. It's sweet to think he may be worried about my reputation.

"Please, have a seat," he says. Only now I notice the jar and glasses on the table between the chairs. "I've brought some of my mother's cider. It's fresh from berries picked last week."

"I'd love some, thank you." I sit as he pours my glass, and I take a sip. I've never had anything but apple cider before, but the strawberry flavor is tart and sweet at the same time. "This is delicious."

"I'm glad you like it," he says. "My mother has a knack for making cider."

"Yes, she does," I agree.

I smile, staring blankly at my glass as I swirl the cider around. I've thought of a million ways to tell Eric about the battle and what he needs to do to stay safe, but none of it feels right now. A part of me screams to just tell him, 'I'm from the future, and you won't make it through the Battle of Bunker Hill,' but I don't. That sounds crazy, even to me. Instead, I stick with the pleasantries while my mind races. "Is Luke feeling well?" I ask.

"He is," he says, taking a sip of his drink. "With many thanks to you."

"You saved him, too," I insist. "Nothing I did would have worked if you hadn't pulled him out so soon."

"It is a blessing I was able to locate him." He gazes at me, the same apprehension I saw in those chocolate orbs that day on the shore faintly noticeable now. "My family owes you a debt of gratitude."

"It was nothing," I say with a shrug. "I'm just glad he's okay."

We're silent for a moment, sipping cider and listening to the stillness of the forest night. "Your cottage is coming along well," I say after a while. *Why can't I just tell him?*

"Yes." He smiles with pride. "It's almost complete."

A stabbing ache wells up inside me thinking about how little time he really has, and how he will never enjoy his cottage. I can't put this off any longer. I have to warn him in a way so that he won't think I'm insane. "I've heard the British are very close," I begin. "There might be a battle soon."

The smile fades from his lips. "Indeed, though we do not know when. You will be safe, however. Please do not worry."

It's way too late for that. "You intend to go, don't you?" I ask.

"Of course," he replies. "This is a battle for our liberty. I must answer the call."

I suck in a deep breath before I blurt out, "I don't think you should go." I look directly at him, my eyes slightly narrowed, knowing that alone won't be enough to stop him. I remember the way he jumped into the water for Luke. He'll feel the same way about this battle. I have to give him a reason not to go, but I still don't know how to say it.

He meets my eyes and softens his gaze. "Fighting is not what any of us wish to do," he says gently. "But this is the only path to freedom. I have no choice but to join the others in battle."

"I know you feel compelled to be there, but I don't think you should be in this particular battle," I tell him. "I have a feeling this one is going to be extremely dangerous, and you could lose your life."

He nods lightly. "It is a risk I am willing to take for liberty," he insists. "It is kind of you to be concerned for me, but I am experienced in battle, as are all my compatriots. This battle is no different."

"But it is different," I argue. How am I going to explain this? "This one is closer to home." I know the minute it comes out of my mouth that it's not going to convince him. I put my hand in my lap, feeling the paper in my dress pocket. If anything, that'll make him want to go even more.

"Hattie," he begins, forgetting the formalities. I look at him, my breath catching in my throat at his intense gaze. "Being close to home is all the more reason to fight. I must protect the people I care about."

I knew he was going to say that. I swallow back the lump in my throat. *Am I one of the people he cares about?* Either way, I can't let him go off to battle and die. I set down my glass and blurt it all out. "Eric, the battle is going to happen sooner than you think. They've already decided to call in the militia today. They'll come for you soon, and the battle will start on Saturday. Please, you can't be at the Battle of Bunker Hill."

His forehead knits together. "What do you mean? How do you know it will be Saturday?"

"I-I just do, that's all," I insist, knowing that won't be enough of an answer for him. "Please promise me you won't go."

He shakes his head. "I must go, Hattie. Tell me where you learned of this. None of us have heard of a battle beginning as soon as Saturday."

"I just know," I insist. "And it's not going to go well… for you. I mean, the British will win the battle, and there will be many casualties. Eric, please, sit this one out. I'm begging you."

"How can you possibly know the outcome?" he asks. "How do you know the name of the battle? That is never established until the fighting is done."

"I just do," I insist.

But that just makes him furrow his brow tighter. "Hattie, please tell me where you're getting your information." he pleads. "Yes, there have been rumors about fighting near the British ships. But no one knows what will happen. We have a strong militia, and it's not impossible that we'll be victorious."

"You don't get it." I inhale, and he looks at me the way everyone here does when my words don't make sense. But none of this is going to make sense anyway, and I have to convince him not to go. I pull out my uncle's map and set it on the table, spreading it out to reveal the side with the battle drawn in detail. "This is the Charleston area," I explain. "This is Breed's Hill, and this is Bunker Hill."

His jaw drops as he scoots forward to look at the map, then back at me. "Hattie—"

But I just keep talking. "This is the first wave," I explain, showing where the British will attack first. "The colonial army will do well, though there are casualties on both sides. The second wave comes from here." I put my finger on the map. "Again, the colonists will surprise the British with how many casualties they are able to inflict. The problem comes on the third wave, from here."

I look up at him finally. His mouth hangs half open, his eyes wide. "How is it possible that you—"

But I don't let him finish. "Eric, your militia will be out of ammunition by then. It'll be a massacre, and if you're there, you're going to be in the middle of it. I can't let you do it. I can't let you go."

"Where did you get this map?" he asks softly.

"It doesn't matter where, but this is how it will happen." I look up at him again. "You have to trust me."

"I want to, Hattie, but this is—" He picks up the map and examines it carefully. "I don't know what to think about this."

"Promise me you'll at least think about it." I swallow again, my throat tight. He hasn't asked me if I'm a spy for the British the way that Charlie did, but I have to wonder if he's thinking it.

He's quiet for a moment, looking at the map again. "I will promise to keep all this in mind," he says finally.

"That's all I can ask for now."

"Hattie, I—" he begins, but his words dissolve into silence, and his eyes lock on mine. I take a stuttering breath. We're so close together now I could easily reach over and pull him toward me. I don't, though. I can't make him think I've completely lost my mind.

After a beat, he looks away. "It is late," he says. "Perhaps I should get you back home to the Monroes." He stands, offering me his elbow.

I get up and wrap my hand around his arm, feeling tiny sparks of electric energy at his touch. He gives me a warm, empathetic smile that tells me he doesn't think I'm lying or crazy. But he doesn't seem to completely believe me, either. I can't blame him.

He starts to lead me down the forest path, the moonlight so bright, we cast shadows on the ground in front of us. I look up at his profile, his strong jawline set firmly ahead. He turns toward my gaze.

"Despite the disappointing news you've enlightened me with regarding the British, I have enjoyed our evening together," he says, his voice deep.

Goosebumps form on my arms. "So have I." Heat rises in my cheeks, and I hope he doesn't notice in the moonlight.

"What are your plans for the future?" he asks.

A pleasant tingle runs down the nape of my neck. Why is he asking? "What do you mean?" I ask finally.

"Will you continue to stay with the Monroes?" he clarifies.

"Oh." I turn my gaze toward the path in front of us. "Yes, that's my plan for now."

"I was hoping you would say that." His tone is different, softer, and my breath catches in my throat.

"I hope we can talk again. Soon. Perhaps about… more pleasant topics." I look at him out of the corner of my eye, wondering if he's beginning to feel the same way I am, like maybe there is a connection between us, something that transcends time.

My arm is still locked around his elbow when he pulls me a little closer and trails his fingers over my arm lightly, leaving me gasping for air. "I should hope we will have plenty of time for more evenings together." I catch a glimpse of the relaxed smile on his face as we continue walking.

But we don't have plenty of time, and the knot in my stomach tightens at the thought. In just a few days, he'll go out to battle, never to return. Never to live a single day in the cottage he built with his highly skilled hands.

My heart starts racing as panic floods my mind. We only have days left together. How is that fair? Why do I have just a few hours to spend with a man I've come so far back in time to find? I have to make the most of our time. I have to grasp these few moments with him… this moment.

"Wait," I say suddenly.

He stops quickly, drops my arm, and turns to me, concern

clouding his face. Standing on my toes, I wrap both arms around his neck. His eyes widen in surprise, but I don't let that stop me, leaning up and softly pressing my lips to his.

He freezes, unsure what to do. I can't blame him. If he didn't think I was crazy before, he certainly must now.

"Desperate times call for desperate measures," I whisper.

Eric stares at me, unblinking for several seconds as my heart hammers in my chest. Then, slowly, the corner of his mouth pulls up into a crooked grin. He lowers his head, and I come up to meet him, my eyes closing as I focus on the feel of him, the faint taste of strawberries lingering on his tongue, the way his breath hitches when I part my lips.

With his arms wrapped tightly around me, I savor this moment as if it's the only one we'll ever get–because it just might be.

CHAPTER FOURTEEN

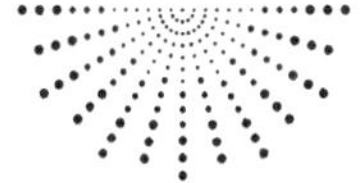

HATTIE

I DON'T WANT TO LET GO. HIS LIPS ON MINE, HIS ARMS AROUND ME, gently caressing my back—I want to stay this way forever. But gradually, we ease out of the deep kiss, savoring those last few seconds before parting.

His brown eyes glisten in the moonlight as he looks at me, his hands still resting gently on my waist. "Hattie," he says with such reverence, his voice husky and soothing. He lifts a hand to run his palm along my cheek.

"Eric." The weight of the war and his impending fate can't reach me now. That dark cloud can wash over me later. Right now, it's all been replaced by a sense of warmth enveloping me, pulsating deep below my skin.

He pulls his hand away from my body reluctantly but immediately takes my hand in his. "How did you have the courage to kiss me?"

"Didn't you want me to?" I ask, hoping I didn't mistake the desire I thought I saw in his eyes.

He chuckles lightly and squeezes my hand. "More than anything. It's just… I've never known a woman to be so forward. That's all."

I hush him playfully, placing my finger on his warm lips. "I come from a place where it's okay for the woman to make the first move," I explain mischievously.

"Where are you from exactly?" he asks. "You don't seem to have a French accent." He winks at me, teasing me in return.

I can't help but giggle, pulling him closer to me. The scent of leather, pine and sage mingles as I breathe him in.

However, being this close to him now reminds me that it won't always be this way. Now, A sense of dread settles over me as I remember he said he had to fight at Bunker Hill. "We have so much more to talk about," I say, "and such little time."

He pulls me into a gentle embrace, holding me close before stepping back. With a soft touch, he lifts my chin, guiding my gaze to his. "We will have plenty of time after the war to be together."

A lump forms in my throat, and I can't respond. We won't have any time if he doesn't survive–or if I go back to the future without him.

"But it is late now, and you should return to the Monroes'," he continues, offering his elbow again. I take it, leaning into him as we make our way down the path where the forest gives way to the Monroe gardens. Rose bushes line the walkway, their petals glowing in the soft moonlight.

"Goodbye until tomorrow, Miss Miller," he says when we reach the end of the walkway. I want to kiss him again, and I can see by the softening of his eyes that he wants the same. Instead, he tilts his head slightly toward the Monroes' back porch, where Charlie sits.

I nod with understanding. "Goodbye until tomorrow, Mr. Thomas."

The evening breeze slips between us like a secret, cool against our warm hands as we finally part. I walk slowly toward Charlie, but turn around midway to look at Eric again. He stands firmly where I left him, shoulders squared, eyes fixed on me, like I'm his anchor in choppy seas.

When I turn back around, Charlie is on her feet, bouncing with a broad smile on her face. Reluctantly, I leave Eric behind and walk toward her. "You must tell me all about your evening, but we had better go to my room first."

I chuckle as she quietly opens the back door and tiptoes in. I turn around one more time, placing one hand on the door to close it behind us. Eric is still waiting there, making sure I'm safely inside. I smile at him again and with one last wave, follow Charlie inside.

It takes two hands to click the heavy door closed without making too much noise. Charlie and I freeze in place for a few beats to be sure no one comes to investigate. She nods finally, waving me forward as we glide up the stairs. I'm glad that the first one isn't as creaky as it will be in the future.

The moment we are in the privacy of her room, she sits on the edge of the bed, leaning forward and pulling me by both arms to sit next to her. "Well?" she asks in an excited whisper. "How was your evening? Don't leave anything out!"

I probably won't tell her everything, given the circumstances, but I launch into what I am comfortable telling her. "He brought delicious strawberry cider his mother had made, and we sat on his porch and talked," I explain quietly, pulling the map out of my pocket. "I showed it to him and explained how the battle will unfold, but frankly, I don't think he believed me."

"He has to believe you," she insists, shaking her head.

"I know." I look down at the map. "I need more time to talk to him. This is too much to explain at once."

"It is." She scoots back in the bed, leaning against the headboard, hugging her knees "But I believe you, so hopefully, you can convince him, too."

"Maybe," I reply. "But he didn't see me suddenly down in what had been an empty hole wearing clothes from 2025."

"That's true." She rests her chin on her knees, her eyes thoughtful. "But I think he will still believe you. He probably wants to talk to you more. Maybe he'll be there tomorrow night waiting for you."

My heart skips a beat at the thought. "Do you think so?"

She sits up straighter and shrugs. "I am certain you will have another opportunity to speak with him. Wouldn't it be romantic if you journeyed over there to his cabin tomorrow night, and he was sitting there waiting for you?"

I nod slowly, folding up the map and putting it back in my pocket. I'll need to show it to him the next time I get a chance.

"He certainly looked at you with fondness," she adds.

I look up, and Charlie gives me a sly smile. "I suppose he did," I admit. If only she knew about the kiss–but I'll keep that part to myself. No reason to scandalize her.

She scoots up closer, holding a pillow to her chest as she settles beside me. "I saw that he was holding your hand. Did he tell you he was fond of you?"

"Not exactly...."

"What does that mean?" she asks. "Did he say it or not?"

"No, but he didn't have to." I feel my face turning a dark shade of red and hope she doesn't notice.

Charlie isn't one to just let the statement go. "Whatever do you mean? What happened, Hattie? You must tell me."

I take a deep breath, telling myself I'll make something out. But when I start talking, the truth comes out. "I kissed him."

Her eyes widen in shock. "You kissed him?"

My face is on fire. "Yep."

She falls back on the bed, tossing the pillow aside dramatically. "Oh, my, Hattie! Whatever did he think of that?"

"He was surprised," I admit. "But he liked it. I told him it's okay where I come from for ladies to be so forward, and he believed me." Why was that so easy for him to believe but not the part about the battle and his impending death?

"This gives me new hope for the future," she says. "How wonderful that a woman can be the one to let a man know her intentions instead of waiting for him. Not that I'm in any hurry. It's just amazing to me that a woman can have such freedom."

I have to agree.

THE NEXT DAY, WE ARE JUST FINISHING BREAKFAST WHEN CHARLIE'S father turns to us, a deep crease of concern marking his expression. "Charlie, Hattie, I'd like to spend the day showing you something," he says. He softens his gaze as he looks at me. "I don't want to worry you, Hattie. But if there is trouble, I want to be sure you know how to defend yourself."

I nod gravely, imagining the heavy weight on his shoulders. At his age, I know he probably won't actually fight in the battle, but I'm fairly sure he will have some involvement. Regardless, he couldn't always be home to protect his family, and John would be on the battlefield.

"I appreciate that," I say, rising from my seat at the table.

"Could I speak to you a moment first?" Mrs. Monroe asks me kindly.

"Of course," I reply.

She directs the younger children to play outside close to the house and leads me into the parlor where we both sit on the sofa. "We haven't had many chances to speak," she says.

"We haven't," I agree, smoothing out my gown.

She smiles warmly. "I wanted to tell you how much I appreciate you spending so much time with Charlie. She has become fond of you, and I can see that's well deserved."

"I really like her a lot," I reply. "Charlie is an amazing girl. I have so much respect for her, and for you and Mr. Monroe for raising her to follow her heart so freely."

"Her father and I have always been proud of her independence," she says. She bites her bottom lip with a gentle smirk. "Frankly, she reminds me of my grandmother. She was always such a feisty soul."

"I'm sure she was wonderful." I smile, wondering what she was like.

"She was." Her eyes focus on a spot across the room, clearly lost in memory. But then she turns back to me. "I just want you to know that if you need anything at all, please tell me. My husband and I are happy to have you here, and we want you to be comfortable."

"I appreciate you both so much," I assure her. "I have everything I need, but I will let you know if there is anything else."

She stands, brushing the wrinkles from her skirt. "Very well, dear. I won't keep you from Mr. Monroe's plans for the day. I admit, it's a frightening situation, but we do need to be able to protect ourselves."

"I understand," I say. "Thank you for speaking to me."

"You're welcome." She gives me a nurturing smile, and my heart aches for my mother.

I haven't thought much about going home since I went to see Eric last night. After our kiss, I don't know what to think. I hope I can save him. All of this puts both of us in such a precarious situation. I'd be lying to myself if I said I wasn't starting to fall for him. He's such a handsome man–so kind, intelligent, and dashing. With his lips on mine, it was clear he has more than just a passing interest in me as well.

It's almost like I've fallen into a romance novel. Reading them always made me long for that sort of deep romance from days gone by. Now, here I am, seeing that it's real.

Too real, honestly. If he dies, what will I do? Or what if I have to go back to the future and leave him behind?

My head begins to spin as I grow more and more overwhelmed. I take a deep breath and go outside to where Mr. Monroe and Charlie wait for me.

"Ah, there you are," he says, leading us to a shed where he shows me how to unhook the many locks he's installed. I inhale sharply when we step inside and see the reason for his precautions. Rifles and other weapons line the walls, more than enough to arm the entire Monroe family and then some.

"Have you handled a rifle before?" he asks.

I shake my head. Even if I had, it would have been nothing like these.

He takes down a musket. "The first step is loading it," he explains, taking his time to show how to open the pan of the gun, pour in gunpowder, load the lead ball cartridge, and pack it with the rammer. He has me do the same with a different musket from his collection, and though it's awkward, I manage, considerably slower than Charlie handles hers. I wonder how often she's done it before and remember her desire to join the men in battle.

Every hair stands up on the back of my neck at the thought.

We head outside where we use a distant tree as a target. I miss by a mile on my first try, of course, then go through the loading process again. How terrifying it must be, hurrying through these steps while the enemy advances.

The rock-hard lump in my chest weighs heavily on me as I think of all these men I've met going off to battle–especially Eric.

Eventually, I get to where I can reasonably hit something. Then we move to the other weapons, first an axe, then a dagger. Mr. Monroe shows us various defensive moves. I'm a little more comfortable following his instructions for these because it's not so complicated. I can't even imagine having to slice into another human being with a sharp object, though. The thought makes my stomach twist.

Eventually, Mrs. Monroe appears on the back porch, waving us inside. Her husband gives her a nod and turns to me. "You did well today, Miss Miller," he says. "It may seem strange for a lady to handle weapons, but I want you both to be ready for anything."

"I am, Father," Charlie chimes in.

I can't be as confident, but I appreciate his efforts. "Thank you for teaching me. I know I have a lot to learn."

"I meant it when I said you did well," he insists. "We will take more time to practice in the coming days. Before we go inside, let me show you one more thing." We go back into the shed where he hands Charlie a knife. "I know you already keep one on you at all times, but I want you to have another, just in case." He turns to me. "Miss Miller, please take this." He pulls a dagger with a holster from the shelf nearby. "You can wear this around your waist beneath your outer garments. Please keep that with you constantly, for the time being."

I nod, knowing how little time we have before another battle breaks out. I can't be sure, but I think I read something in his eyes telling me he knows this, too. Perhaps he was with the leaders who heard the news about the British. I may never know. "Thank you," I tell him.

He gives me a reassuring pat on the shoulder, but my hands shake as I take the dagger from him and adjust it around my waist, tucking it under my top skirt. Anxiety gnaws at me, awakening fear in every nerve in my body. Next to me, Charlie looks calm, determined, and it reminds me that I absolutely do not belong here.

The closest I've ever come to battle is watching an ex-boyfriend play a stupid video game. Now, I might just be thrown into it.

More than ever, I want to go home.

CHAPTER FIFTEEN

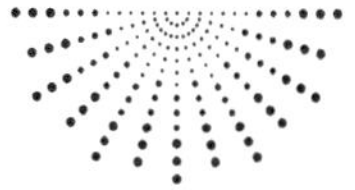

Under the shade of a sturdy oak tree, a cool breeze rushes over my forehead. It draws my attention away from applying the final coat of wax to my dining room table. I use the moment to admire the house I've been building for so long, and then my thoughts drift to Hattie.

I can almost feel the heat of her presence, that wild energy radiating from her. Hattie's red hair—bold and untamed. It's flame-like in the way it catches the light, and makes me want to run my fingers through it, and see how it tangles between them.

I imagine the way she looks when she laughs, head thrown back, eyes sparkling with mischief and something deeper, something I'm not sure I can name. Something otherworldly.

Her skin is warm under my touch, smooth, and I picture the intensity in her eyes when she gets close to me. Hattie is the kind of woman who knows exactly what she wants and doesn't settle for anything less. I could tell that the moment we kissed.

I can't help but smile at the recollection of last night when she kissed me. A woman who kisses a man first must be so bold to do so.

I've never heard of such a thing, but then, I've never met anyone like her. Yet, I imagine my future with her.

The taste of her lips lingers, and holding her in my arms felt like the world finally clicked into place, like she'd always belonged there. The way her body fit perfectly against mine was effortless, like we were two pieces of a puzzle. Even the smallest touch, the brush of her fingertips across my skin, sent a surge of heat straight to my chest. When her elbow locked in mine, it was more than just physical; it was a raw connection. Every inch of her, every movement, made it clear that this was where she was meant to be, right here, with me.

What is this feeling that overcomes me not only in her presence, but with the mere thought of her? I am fond of her, drawn to her, yet this seems like so much more. It is not the first time I've imagined her sharing this home with me. I have never considered married life with any other woman.

Is this love?

Perhaps it is, yet so much about Hattie perplexes me. She speaks of the future with such certainty, it's as though she has seen it with her own eyes. It is simply not possible to know even the name of the battle, let alone the exact place it will be fought. And claiming to know which side will be victorious? Preposterous! Yet, she spoke every word of future battle as though it were fact.

It's possible, even likely, that she's a British spy, or some kind of undercover soldier, planted here with the Monroes. No one would guess a woman would be a soldier or a spy, and the thought has gnawed at the back of my mind since last night when she showed me the map. If she's playing a game with me, I'm not sure if I'm the pawn or the player.

I try to shake the thought, returning to my work, ensuring each fold of the beveled edge is properly covered in wax.

Moments later, I'm interrupted again, this time not by my own thoughts but by the thud of horse hooves rapidly approaching. I recognize Levi's figure from afar, but as he nears, a lump in my throat forms at his urgent, troubled expression.

"I bring news of the war," he says, dismounting.

Hattie's warnings flood my mind.

"We have received orders," he continues, removing his hat to wipe his brow. "There are rumors of British troops amassing to surround the city. The militia leaders find these reports credible."

I nod firmly, but my heart hammers against my ribcage. "Where are we needed?"

"We'll be receiving orders at the meeting place within the week," he explains.

A shiver shoots down my spine. Hattie knew the battle would be coming soon. How is that possible? Who does she know, and how high are they ranked? Who drew that map?

"Eric?"

I steel myself against a shudder. "Have you alerted the Monroes?"

"Not yet," he says, sliding his foot into the stirrup and mounting his horse.

I mount mine as well. "I'll tell them," I insist. "Warn the other neighbors. We'll meet back home to discuss this further."

"Consider it done," he says, turning his horse as I start riding toward the Monroe estate. "And Eric—this is it, isn't it?" Levi asks. "We'll finally drive off the British?"

The British will win. Hattie's words echo in my mind. "We will," I say instead.

He gives me a firm nod and gathers the bridle, pressing the horse into a full gallop toward the Robinson property. I turn my attention toward the Monroe house and ride off.

Fortunately, I find John outside replacing wood on his wellhead so I can deliver the news to him alone first.

He stops his work as I approach, the weight of concern heavy in his eyes, much as I must have looked when Levi rode out to me. "We've been called," he says with certainty, not a question, but a statement.

"We have," I confirm. "We must be at the meeting place within the week. We have mere days." I cannot help the somber tone in my voice.

"That is soon. This one feels close to home with all the commotion in the harbor." He rubs his chin thoughtfully.

"Levi is informing the other neighbors. I wanted to tell you as soon as I heard."

"My father has business in the city, but my mother is inside the house. I believe I heard Miss Miller, Charlie, and the children's voices around here earlier." John and I begin to walk toward his house.

My breath catches in my throat at the thought of seeing Hattie again. Sweet memories of her lips against mine creep into my mind, but they are intertwined with dread and confusion. She has either predicted this battle... or she is working with someone who has information I don't have. What confuses me even more is that she has asked that I avoid the battle.

I must fulfill my duty to the militia, to my fellow colonists dreaming of liberty. But such a large part of me longs for many more relaxed, quiet evenings alone with Hattie on my porch.

We find Charlie and Hattie playing a game of ninepins with John's younger siblings. For a moment, I stand back, watching Hattie with the Monroe children. She is naturally nurturing, her laughter ringing through the air as she takes her turn, effortlessly rolling the ball down the worn dirt lane. There is something about the way she moves. She is graceful and confident. She demands my attention every time I am around her.

The children cheer as she knocks down almost every pin with a single roll, and I can't help but admire how she interacts with them, how she bridges the gap between being a beautiful woman and a playful, carefree spirit.

As John and I approach, the children notice and happily bombard us with the score and details of the game. We exchange feigned interest for their good spirits, and John asks Charlie to have a private word.

I use the opportunity to step away from the children with Hattie for a quiet moment.

"You were correct," I whisper, "about the time and place of the upcoming battle."

Her blue eyes soften. "This is exactly how it happened," she murmurs, not looking directly at me. I tilt my head at the strange choice of past tense, and she corrects herself. "It's how it's going to happen. Eric, that's why I don't want you to go. You need to sit this battle out."

Hattie looks at the children who are still playing their game and are paying no attention to us. She grips my hand tightly, and I can feel the tension in her, the way she's holding herself back.

"I understand," I try to explain, shaking my head. "I don't want to leave you. But I'm not leaving you behind, either. I'll be back as soon as possible. And I'm going to do everything I can to make sure I come back in one piece."

A tear rolls down Hattie's cheek, and I fear I might lose my composure as well.

I pause for a second, letting out a breath. "I know it's not fair, but... I need you to understand. This is something I have to do. I wish I didn't have to go, but I'm not the kind of man who can turn my back on my brothers, friends, and neighbors." I give her a small, shaky smile, trying to reassure her, maybe myself, too. "I just need you to trust me... that I will return."

Just as I'm about to say more, a burst of laughter and cheers from the children cuts through the moment, dragging us both back to reality. I glance over and see them a few feet away, completely caught up in their game, oblivious to everything else. The noise feels almost too loud, too out of place for the quiet moment we were sharing.

Reluctantly dropping her hand, I ask, "Will you meet me tonight at my house in the woods? Midnight?"

She answers immediately, a spark of enthusiasm lighting her eyes. "Yes. I'll be there."

"We will speak then. I must go now." The moment passes, and I have no option but to leave, though I can't bring myself to look away from her.

Eventually, I force myself to turn to John. "I will meet up with you again soon."

Exiting the Monroe yard and mounting my horse, my thoughts drift to my next task. I must warn my family of the impending battle so close to home.

While I am looking forward to spending time with Hattie alone once more, I know it will break her heart when I tell her my decision is final.

It is my duty to fight. I will not change my mind.

CHAPTER SIXTEEN

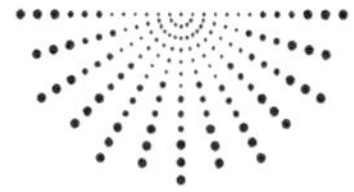

Hattie

It's a quarter to midnight, and June's humidity presses against me like a heavy blanket. The night is thick with the hum of insects, the smell of lavender in the air, and a sentiment I can't shake. It feels like the calm before a storm. If only it were a summer rain shower on the horizon, but that's not what I dread. It's a battle.

Eric asked me to meet him at the cottage tonight at midnight, and it will likely be my last chance to change his mind. To beg him not to fight at Bunker Hill.

As I walk toward the cottage, the world feels suspended, as if time itself has paused. I miss my parents and my sister. I long for home.

Remembering what Aunt Ida said about lives lost in the battle sends a chill up my spine. When she told us the man who built the cottage never returned… something in that moment connected me to Eric in a way I can't explain.

I am unsure of what to expect when I get to Eric's cottage tonight, but I know what's coming. He's going to leave soon, go off to the battle that's already looming. The war is coming, and he's a part of it.

Everyone's lives will be changed forever by what Eric faces on that hill—where he will lose his life. How can I let that happen to him? To his friends and family?

My whole being feels weighed down with that knowledge. I can't stop thinking about what I've told him, the things I hope he's starting to believe about the future. The second real clash of arms in the fight for independence, the courage and the loss that will shape everything. It's all coming, no matter what I say or do.

When I reach his porch, Eric stands in the doorway, waiting for me. Moonlight sweeps across his masculine features, and the butterflies in my stomach flutter wildly.

"It's a beautiful night," I say softly, feeling the words catch in my throat as I step closer to him.

"I had not noticed." His voice is low. He reaches out to stroke my cheek.

"You must be too worried about the battle to have noticed?" I'm puzzled.

"Too distracted by thoughts of you...." He trails off.

I hope it's too dark for Eric to see me blush at his words. He takes my hand, and we step off the porch. He leads me to a table under a large tree.

"I finished the dining table this afternoon," he says. The pale light of the moon shines on us, and I can see a fleeting moment of pride wash over his face.

"You made this yourself?" I marvel. The men I've dated in the past... or the future... either way, they didn't know how to make their own sandwich, let alone build their own furniture. "It's incredible."

"Thank you." He takes a deep breath. "I need to speak with you." His voice cracks with emotion. "I leave soon. The battle is almost here."

"I know," I say quietly. "I know you're planning to go. But you can't. You just can't. Eric, you will not come back...."

He steps closer, cutting me off. His hand comes up to lift my chin, and for a split second, everything feels less terrifying.

"I've been thinking about everything you've said," Eric murmurs, his thumb brushing along my jaw. "About the war. About the future. I still don't know how you know, and part of me thinks that maybe you're—Hattie, are you an enemy spy?" he asks, searching my face.

Not only does he fail to understand that I'm telling him his fate—*that he's going to die in battle*—but he thinks I'm a British spy? For a heartbeat, the weight of the war, the death, the destruction, all of it, feels so distant. It seems almost laughable, the idea that I could be a spy for the enemy. How absurd.

And yet, the truth is even more ridiculous. I'm a time traveler, stranded in a world that isn't mine, trying to figure out how to protect him. I can't help it. I start to giggle. The sound bubbles up, jagged laughter, at the madness of the whole situation.

Eric watches me, his brow furrowed in concern, as I cackle. I wish I could explain, but how do you explain something so impossible?

I stop giggling, a little embarrassed, and catch my breath. Eric is clearly worried.

"What is so humorous?" he asks.

"Eric, I promise I'm not a spy. I'm just a woman with a map. I'm worried about all of us, especially you," I whisper, reaching for him.

Pulling me into an embrace, my face against his chest, he murmurs over the top of my head, "I need you to know something, Hattie. No matter what happens, I... I don't want to go into that battle unsure of what I'm leaving behind."

My heartbeat quickens. I don't have the words for what I'm feeling. Eric is worried about leaving me, of all people. He should be fearful for his life. Instead, he's concerned about my feelings–our potential future. He's about to march into something that will change everything, and I don't know if I can stop it.

But then, I'm not sure that I should. What if I change history? What if I'm never able to return home? Should I even try to stop him?

Of course I should. I can't stand here, at this moment, holding back. Not with him. Not when I feel such a connection to him.

Before either of us can say another word, I press my lips to his. It's a kiss of passion and need. An unspoken plea that says everything we're both too afraid to speak aloud. Longing surges within me the second I feel his hands wrap around my waist.

"I don't want to lose you," I say, looking up at him.

Eric's eyes darken with something fierce and fragile all at once.

Without speaking, I take his hand and lead him to a nearby tree with low hanging branches and a bank of moss beneath it.

Frantically, we shed our clothes, fingers fumbling over buttons and the endless layers this era insists upon. At last, my gaze drinks in Eric's bare, chiseled form. He is the very embodiment of all any woman would desire; sculpted arms seemingly crafted for the sole purpose of holding me, a chiseled chest, and eyes so deep and haunting, I can't help but sink into them.

I lower myself to the ground and pull Eric down to meet me. He's gentle at first, as if testing the waters. I can't blame him for being unsure. I'm honestly surprised we've gotten this far.

"Are you certain you want this, Hattie?" he asks, his voice low and uncertain. And in that moment, I see his vulnerability. For him, this is unfamiliar terrain. In this time, sex isn't something proper young women experience outside of marriage. The weight of that realization settles between us, tender and real.

But this is a time of war, and neither of us knows what tomorrow may bring. That much, he can certainly understand.

"I've never been more certain of anything in my life," I whisper, pressing my lips to his again.

Then Eric claims me, too—not with haste, but with a reverence that steals my breath. His lips find my neck, and I wrap my arms around him. When he teases the sensitive skin just behind my ear, a moan escapes me, soft, involuntary. In response, his hand slips lower, seeking and finding the part of me already aching, already wet and waiting.

As he enters me, the pleasure is immediate and all-consuming. Eric awakens feelings within me, unlike anything I've ever known. Ecstasy flows through me, fierce and beautiful.

He groans into my neck, and I feel my palms against his tight biceps as though I'm instinctively holding on for dear life. Our bodies find a rhythm older than time. We were made for this moment, for each other.

We reach the peak together, waves of release crashing through us.

Moments pass, as we lie breathless.

Eric finally speaks. "I'm profoundly sorry this happened the way it did, under a tree rather than in the sanctity of a marriage bed." He looks genuinely worried.

I force back another fit of laughter considering the first one seemed to concern him. "Don't be silly," I say. "This was magical. Special."

We share one more deep kiss before rising to redress, and my mind begins to race all over again. I know that I'll have to face what comes next. The battle, my future in the past, and the ache in my heart for the world to which I'm supposed to return.

"I'm not ready for you to leave," I murmur, my voice weak. The fear that has been building in me is real now, raw. "I don't know what's going to happen to you."

Eric pulls me closer, pressing his lips to my forehead. "I'll come back," he says, steadily, like he's trying to convince both of us.

I want to believe him. I need to believe him.

But part of me screams—*I'm not from here*. I'm not supposed to be here. And the moment he leaves for that battle, the one that I know he doesn't return from, I'll be left behind in this world that isn't mine—alone.

And I don't know how I'll be able to let him go.

Not when I love him.

CHAPTER SEVENTEEN

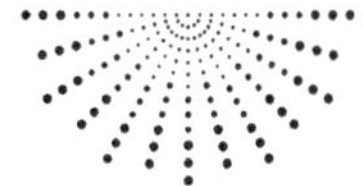

Eric

Thursday morning, I kneel beneath the tree in my yard, where the roots twist like ropes, and my heart still holds the memory of her.

I remember the way Hattie's flame-red hair spread out on the ground last night beneath this old oak tree, the stars barely visible through the branches. Hot summer air threaded with the scent of lavender and earth.

Everything we'd tried to hold back came rushing out in the quiet, in the way her lips found mine. We lay together, and in that moment, nothing else existed. Not war, not duty, not time. Just her, warm and real in my arms. I knew then how much that memory would matter and that I would carry it with me into battle.

The stone here under the tree is flat and half-buried, just as I left it. My name, *ERIC,* is already carved deep into the surface, sharp lines I etched months ago when I chose a place to build my little house.

Now I add hers.

& HATTIE

Each tap of the chisel feels like a vow. Even if I don't make it back from the fight that's coming, I need this to be here. I need it to say that once, even if just for a little while, I loved her and she loved me.

I hope, God willing, we still have more time, and we can make real vows to each other, witnessed by our family and friends.

I sit back on my heels admiring my work. The wind rustles the branches overhead. I touch the rough sandstone once more, then rise, mount my horse, and head toward the Monroe house.

When I arrive, John and his family are in the backyard. It looks as though he has just finished strapping on his musket, and Mrs. Monroe's arms are locked around him. She cries silently into his chest.

I swallow hard at the somber scene. Mr. Monroe looks as though he wants to take his son's place, and Charlie and the children are weeping.

Hattie stands nearby. Her eyes, rimmed in pink and swollen, meet mine, and I see that same fear in them. Underneath the fear, I see something else. Resolve. She's already told me so much about the battle, and now I can tell, she's going to try, once again, to keep me from leaving.

I dismount, nod at John, and then Hattie and I give the Monroes some space.

She wastes no time. No pleasantries. No greeting. The moment I approach, she pulls the map from the pocket of her dress and unfolds it, her fingers trembling with urgency. "Eric," she says, her voice sharp, "they'll come by boat on Saturday morning," she says quietly but with such certainty, I know she believes every word. "The first and second waves will be bloody, but your men will still have gunpowder. It's the third wave you have to worry about. You'll be nearly out of ammunition by then. That's when they'll push the hardest."

I look at the map, then at her, and I'm still just as confused as the first time I saw it. "How do you know this? Who gave you this map, Hattie?"

She hesitates, then shakes her head. "You don't want me to answer that."

"I certainly do."

Her voice is soft but sure. "I can't explain how I know or who I got it from. You won't believe me. I just know. Please, Eric. Remember what I'm telling you."

There's no reason I should believe her. No logic that explains how she knows this. And yet, I do. With everything in me–and I no longer believe there's a possibility of her being a spy.

"I trust you," I say. "With my life."

Her eyes fill with tears. "Then stay safe. Promise me."

"I promise I'll try."

I wish I could kiss her one last time. A deep kiss, like we've run out of time, because maybe we have. Alas, John's family would witness our kiss, and it wouldn't be proper. Especially when their son is leaving for war.

When we part, Hattie begins to sob.

By early afternoon, I'm with my brothers, Colin and Levi, and John Monroe, headed on foot toward the meeting place. Riding our horses would give away our position to the enemy.

We were instructed to meet at a small church tucked into the woods about five miles away from the hills on Hattie's map. We will gather here, awaiting our next orders.

Deep in thought, the four of us walk in silence. Every step seems heavier than the last. I feel like all the things that used to matter–chores, fences, tables—don't anymore. Now, all that matters is my pledge to my country and returning to Hattie–unharmed.

Even now, we are so close to the land, the hills, drawn on her map, and it will make sense to fortify the high ground....

I break the silence, my voice slipping out before I can stop it. "George Bunker and Ebenezer Breed."

My friend and brothers look at me as though I've lost my mind. "Pray, do you mind expanding on that?" Colin asks with a mischievous glint in his eye.

Having not meant to mention anything Hattie told me, I rush to think of something, anything, to explain. Clearing my throat and stammering, "I, uh, believe that is who owns the land where we will be stationed."

Colin and Levi look at one another and back at me, perplexed.

"Could be," John offers. "That is the area near the harbor. Mr. Breed does business with my father."

Wanting to change the subject and having still not regained my self-control, I swallow hard and blurt out, "I'm going to ask her to marry me."

"Who? The Miller girl?" John asks.

"If I make it through this battle, yes." I reply.

Colin whistles.

Levi grins and claps me on the back. "About time you chose a wife!"

I smile, but it's thin. My guts are twisted in knots. What if I don't make it home to her?

That night, we sleep in the church. The pews and floor are hard, the air humid, and no one truly rests. Some men take shifts guarding the doors, muskets across their laps, eyes heavy. Others are stationed outside, hidden in the trees, watching the roads and the dark edges of the woods for any sign of movement. The quiet, or what passes for it, is broken only by the occasional cough, the creak of floorboards, or the low hum of whispered prayers. We are all waiting.

Levi snores nearby, and I lie flat on my back, staring up at the low ceiling.

I think about what Hattie said. The third wave. The ammunition running dry.

I could warn my brothers, my friends. But what would I say? That Hattie *knows* the future? That she *knows* what's coming?

They'd look at me like I needed to be escorted to the doctor to have my head examined. They proved that when I simply mentioned the ground we'll be stationed on.

How can I tell them the exact turn of events without them thinking I'm losing my grip on reality? Or worse, they'll think I'm being superstitious. The kind of man who sees omens in bird flight patterns and hears the fate of men singing in the wind.

If I speak and I'm wrong, I'll lose their trust. If I hold my tongue, and she's right....

I don't know what to do. My heart pulls one way. My head pulls the other.

But if there's a chance, even the smallest one, that she's right... can I really afford not to believe her? At what cost?

John has always trusted me. And Colin and Levi would follow me into the fire. Yet, a part of me wonders, what if I speak and they laugh it off?

And yet... how can I *not* tell them? If Hattie's right, and I say nothing, and one of them dies....

God, how would I live with myself after that?

I have one more day. One more day to decide whether to stay silent or to tell them what Hattie has shared with me. I'm not a coward, but this choice, this impossible yoke, it makes me feel like one.

I close my eyes, but her voice echoes in my mind: *"The third wave... you'll be out of ammunition... they'll push back even harder...."*

I don't know if I can carry this knowledge, this burden, alone.

Sleep pulls at me slowly. My head begins to ache from the weight of what tomorrow and the coming days might bring, but fortunately, my mind begins to slip elsewhere... back to her.

Back to under the old tree....

We didn't rush. It was as if we both knew the moment wouldn't last, and we were trying to stretch it out, make time forget itself. Her hands were gentle, but her eyes, God, her beautiful eyes ignited within me something fierce.

We made love slowly, like it was sacred. Like if we moved too fast, it might vanish. I didn't want to leave her. I still don't.

Now, in the dark church, I press my hand to my chest and vow to return from this battle alive.

If for no other reason, no one else, then for Hattie.

CHAPTER EIGHTEEN

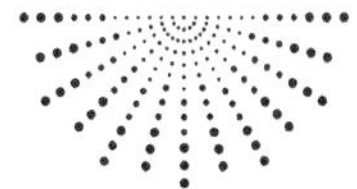

Friday morning, I feel like I'm walking under water. Every breath takes so much more effort than it should. Each moment presses against me with the weight of inevitability. Inside, I'm unraveling and longing for home. I miss my little sister Nina most of all.

Why am I here if not to change the outcome of the battle? The Battle of Bunker Hill. I know about the high body count, the valor and the tragedy. But none of the textbooks ever mentioned Eric Thomas. None of them said: *And a man with soft brown eyes and a kind, quiet demeanor, died here.*

And now I know tomorrow is the day, and I know Eric Thomas will fight.

Of course he will. He's too brave. Too good. Too stubborn.

I wanted to scream at him to stay home yesterday. I wanted to throw myself at his feet and beg him to be a coward, just this once, so I wouldn't have to lose him. But I didn't. I couldn't. Because even though I've crossed centuries, I can't change who he is.

So, instead of finding him and begging him not to go, today, I help

Mrs. Monroe and Charlie in the kitchen. They are both calm, composed, methodical. I suppose, if we stop going through the motions and allow ourselves a moment, one of us will begin to cry, and that will trigger the other two. We don't want to remind each other of the sadness and the fear, so we measure out rations, tie up bundles of spring vegetables, jerky, hardtack, and cheese with neat loops of twine, like we aren't preparing supplies for men who might not come back home. I try to mimic their steadiness, but every time I tie a bundle, I imagine Eric, John, Colin, and Levi out there on the front lines, and my hands begin to shake.

Charlie must have noticed and breaks the silence when Mrs. Monroe steps outside to check on the children.

"You look like you're going to cry." She gently rubs my arm.

"I'm fine." I try to smile.

"You're not. None of us are fine today." She leans forward, lowering her voice like she is telling me a secret. "I've been thinking."

"Oh, no," I joke.

Charlie grins. "What if we went with them?"

I freeze, hands tightening around the fabric of the bundle I'm holding. "Charlie…."

"We could follow them to the hills. We know what's going to happen already, so we could trail them when they march out in the morning."

"Charlie…."

"I'm serious," she says all too confidently, eyes gleaming. "Eric and John will be there. They'll be on the front lines. You and I, we can fight. Mostly, we can help protect them. Watch their backs. Change what happens."

"Charlie, you're not just being impulsive. You're suggesting we do something that will most definitely end in disaster."

I see the desperation in her eyes. Hope, tangled with disappointment. I know what she's thinking. If we are there, maybe Eric won't die. Like in a fairytale, we could all come home from battle in one piece, but I know better.

"You don't understand," I finally say, my voice cracking. "It'll be chaos. Blood and smoke. Men screaming, body parts flying through the air. They'll be kids, just like you, dying in the mud."

It takes Charlie a moment to respond, and I can see the tears welling up in her eyes.

"I know," she whispers. "I know what kind of battle it is. I just don't want to sit here and wait for them to die."

Her words hit me like a slap. Because that's exactly what I've been doing. Waiting. Bracing. Mourning him before it even happens. I reach out and embrace Charlie.

"You have become like a sister to me in such a short time. I don't know what I would do if you left for that battle and didn't come home…." I trail off upon hearing Mrs. Monroe coming back inside the house. I don't want to worry her even more with the ideas Charlie has rolling around in her mind.

The rest of the day passes in fragments. More food is packed, more wood hauled in, more shallow smiles and quiet nods.

Mr. Monroe and some of the older men go to all of the houses and gather the bundles made by wives and mothers, delivering them to the soldiers by the wagon load at their meeting place.

Under all the chores and mindless work, that question beats like a drum in the back of my mind: *What if we followed them?*

Guilt seeps into my heart.

That night, Charlie and I lay side by side on her goose feather mattress, the scent of which I am finally getting used to.

"We could do it," Charlie whispers again. "We could hide in the forest until the fighting starts. Then find them. Protect them."

I turn my head to look at her. "And what then? If you see a man coming at John with a bayonet, what do you do? Can you stab him? Can you shoot someone? Because if you can't, then you're just another body on that hill. And I can't—I *can't* watch you die, too."

"I'm not afraid," she says.

"You should be."

She reaches out in the dark and takes my hand. "I'm more afraid of losing them than of losing my own life. And Hattie, I feel like I am just as much a militia soldier as any of the men are."

My throat burns as I fight back the tears threatening to spill over in my eyes.

Eventually, Charlie's breathing slows. She falls asleep, hand still tangled with mine.

I roll over and stare at the ceiling, picturing Eric's handsome face in the moonlight. That morphs into images of battle flashing through my reverie, and I must push away thoughts of Eric entirely.

My thoughts turn to the well behind his cottage, the one I fell through to get here. My escape hatch. My way out.

Can I go back through it?

But how can I leave Eric and Charlie behind?

Overwhelmed by emotion, I feel sick.

The nausea rises fast, curling up from deep in my stomach like smoke from a fire I can't put out. I push the blanket off. My feet hit the cool wooden floor, and I move quickly, careful not to wake Charlie as I open the bedroom door and slip out into the narrow hallway.

The house is silent. I go down the stairs and make my way to the back door, fumbling with the latch in the dark. Outside, the air is cooler than I expect, damp, and the scent of wet grass only intensifies the feeling in my gut.

I barely make it past the steps before I double over and vomit into the dirt.

My hands dig into the grass. I brace myself, the tears coming now —hot and silent, carving streaks down my cheeks. I stay there for a long moment, shaking, breath ragged. The earth feels cold beneath my knees, the stars above impossibly still. How dare the sky be so peaceful when everything inside me is unraveling?

When the sickness passes, I move away a bit and sit on the grass. The stars blur through the tears I don't have the energy to wipe away. I clasp my hands in my lap, more from instinct than any practiced belief, and lower my head.

"Please," I whisper. "Please don't let him die." My voice is hoarse, the prayer barely audible. "He's such a good man. He doesn't deserve to be buried on some hill. Please. If anything I do matters… if time can be bent, or rewritten, or bargained with, please let him live."

I wipe my eyes on my sleeve and whisper his name. "Eric."

I can't remember the last time I prayed, but I'm desperate, my knees pressed into the earth and my fingers curled in the hem of my nightdress.

Eventually, I rise slowly, legs stiff, and creep back into the house. The door creaks a little as I shut it behind me, and I hold my breath until I'm sure no one has stirred.

Back in the bedroom, Charlie hasn't moved. She's still on her side, her face relaxed in sleep, the weight of the coming day forgotten for now. One arm is flung over her pillow, her dark hair fanned out around her like a halo. She looks peaceful, like the night sky.

I slide back under the covers beside her, my body still cold, my skin clammy. I wrap the blanket tighter around me, willing the warmth to return.

I watch her for a moment longer, then close my eyes.

Tomorrow is coming fast.

And there's no changing it.

CHAPTER NINETEEN

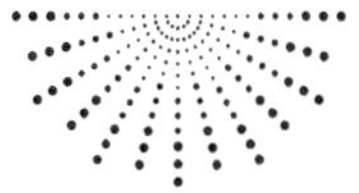

Friday night is hot and still. We wait in the churchyard for word from the top, orders for when and where to move.

Just a couple of hours before midnight, a rider comes galloping up the hill, his horse kicking up dust that glows pale under the moonlight. The news he brings spreads like lightning through the crowd.

"Fortify the high ground." Orders from Colonel William Prescott.

"Men, we are to dig on the hills near the harbor. A wagon load of tools and supplies will be waiting for us when we arrive," he adds.

I grip the handle of my shovel tightly as we march toward the hill. We heard word of militia men coming from all over to fight with us today but as my brothers, John and I look around, we are amazed.

"There must be at least one thousand men here," I marvel.

"Aye, it's a good sight to see. A fine sight to see today," John agrees.

Breed's Hill is steep and muddy, its back bent toward the Charles River. Bunker's Hill looms northwest. We're told to dig in on both, creating an earthen wall of protection.

Armed with pickaxes and shovels, we build a redoubt wall tall enough to hide behind, and then we begin reinforcing the earthen wall with stone and double wooden rails.

Colonel Prescott moves among us, barking orders. "Make it high enough to shield a man reloading!"

Men swing and dig through the night, sweat pouring down like rain even though the sky is clear. Even with mud-caked boots, blistered hands, we dig anyway.

I pause for a breath, wiping my forehead with my sleeve. My hands tremble. Not from fear, not yet, but from the weight of the work, the lack of rest. Still, something else tugs at my heart.

Hattie.

Her message was clear and still lingers in my mind. The British will win the battle. But it will show the colonists how well we can fight, that we have a chance.

She said it with such certainty, as if she'd already seen it happen.

I squeeze my eyes shut. *Please, God,* I whisper. *Let me live. Let my brothers live. Let John live.* I look over and see Colin swinging his pick with fire in his eyes. Levi plunges a wooden stake into the dirt. John is already deep into the trench, working like a man who's never known the meaning of the word tired.

Before we complete our work, I finally bring myself to speak up. "There will be three attacks. On the second one, we move to the back of the line." I try to keep my voice low and steady.

"Have you been sneaking a nip of whiskey, Eric? How could you possibly know that?" Levi asks.

"You must simply trust me and do as I say. After the second attack we will run out of powder. We will not retreat but move to the back of the line to await further orders. Understood?"

Levi, Colin, and John wear the same expression of worry—but they nod, as if trying to convince themselves they can trust me when it matters.

Once we are satisfied we have created something that might just save our lives, we try to get an hour or two of rest before dawn.

THE BRITISH SHIPS IN THE CHARLES RIVER OPEN CANNON FIRE THE moment the sun rises. The booms are so loud they shake the earth beneath my feet. Smoke rolls over the hill like a storm, but we don't flinch. We are ready. We've built the walls. We've laid the dirt. We have our muskets.

"We hold until after the second charge," I say to Levi, Colin, and John once more. We crouch behind the wall, just beneath the ridge. "That's it. Two attacks. Then we move to the back of the line. We can't win this war if we all die here."

"You speak the truth," John calls over the sounds of battle. "Alas, we don't want to back down."

Levi and Colin seem to struggle with the idea of feeling like cowards if we turn around, as well. Their facial expressions and body language scream apprehension.

I don't blame them. Ever since Hattie showed me the map, I've been torn. Do I run and save myself, my brothers, and my best friend, or stay, fight, and die here?

All I can do is hope they trust me enough to follow me when the time comes.

After hours of cannon fire and crouching behind the wall, too leery to so much as peek over, the Robinson brothers finally appear in our section of the redoubt.

"Where have you been? We lost sight of you and thought the worst!" John says, shaking Nathaniel's hand.

"We were nearby. Colonel Gridley is moving men around," he replies.

"Pray tell, how will that help? We are under fire!" Colin shouts.

"Apparently, the British are having trouble with the tide being so low. The river is so shallow this time of day, they can't get their men on shore. It might be noon before we see action," Nathaniel explains.

"It seems like everyone knows the outcome of this battle except for me!" Levi yells over yet another boom.

By the time the sun is high in the sky, the British are landing on the shore—red coats glinting in the sun. They march in lines too neat for this kind of battle.

I crouch low, musket ready. The sound of men praying, cursing, breathing heavy, it all blurs into one hum of dread.

The first wave hits hard, but we're stronger. We fire from the high ground, and they fall like wheat beneath a sickle. Smoke chokes the sky. The roar of muskets and the deep, thunderous pulse of cannon fire turn my bones to ice, but I press forward, musket clutched in my hands.

The British attack a second time, and we hit them with everything we have. The front line of Redcoats collapses, bodies piling on the ground, forcing the second line to step over their fallen.

"Hold your fire!" Colonel Prescott shouts, his voice cutting through the chaos. "Wait 'til you see the whites of their eyes!"

God help us, I can see them now! They're coming in tight, steady lines like they've done this a thousand times.

I check the powder in my pan, heart hammering against my ribs. Sweat pours down my face, stinging my eyes.

Closer.

Closer.

Now!

"Fire!"

Flame and thunder burst from the line. The recoil punches my shoulder; smoke blinds me. I hear men scream, and through the haze I see the second line of British fall.

Reload. Ram the charge. Prime the pan. Fire again.

Everything is motion and madness. Blood. Smoke. Screaming. They're climbing over the wall now.

"They must be low on ammo, too!" I shout to anyone listening.

Our powder's nearly gone. I check my pouch. Two shots. Maybe three.

"We move now," I say.

Colin's eyes are wild. "Now?" he asks.

"Yes. If we stay, we die. If we die, we don't live to fight another day."

I grab Levi's collar and pull him back. John convinces Colin to follow with a word, "Concord."

We slide back through the ranks. Some don't make it—men screaming as they collapse behind us. We don't look. We can't. We head for the grove, hearts pounding.

As I run, I look back once, just once, and I think, what a tragedy it would be to lose this hill. We have the high ground….

We fall all the way back to the rear. Colin, Levi, John, and me, panting, smoke-streaked, hearts thudding like drums. Our hands are blistered from reloading, our shoulders aching from recoil, and our mouths taste like powder and iron.

We duck behind the ridge of the fort, wiping sweat and grime from our eyes, just as a fresh volley crackles above us. Then the sky changes.

"Eric," John breathes, staring past me, his voice hollow. "Look."

I turn. My stomach drops.

Charlestown is burning.

From this hill, we can see it clear as day—flames licking up from rooftops, black smoke curling into the sky like the devil's breath. The British ships have turned their guns on the town. They're not just after us. They're punishing everything that stands.

Colin mutters something I don't catch. Levi stares in stunned silence. I can't tear my eyes away.

The fire spreads fast, devouring houses, shops, churches. My chest tightens. Those were our neighbors. Our streets. I remember walking through Charlestown as a boy, chasing John past bakeries and old brick taverns.

And now…

Gone. Just gone.

"They're burning it all," I say, my voice low, tight with rage. "They'll burn everything before they let it go."

John nods slowly. "Then we can't let them have it."

"I'm out of ammunition. I have nothing left." Levi looks sick.

"Should we fix bayonets?" Colin asks just as we hear the order from Prescott.

"FIX BAYONETS!"

I grip my musket tighter and ready myself for hand to hand combat with men who might still be armed with gunpowder.

I know what's coming next and God help us, none of us are ready for it.

CHAPTER TWENTY

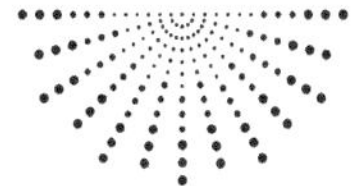

Hattie

Saturday morning, I wake up to what sounds like thunder before the sun has fully risen. I rub my eyes and notice a strange stillness in the room. With a jolt, I gasp at the realization: that's not thunder.

I roll toward the other side of the bed. It's cold. Charlie isn't there.

I sit up slowly, heart pounding, glancing around the room. Maybe she rose early and went downstairs to help Mrs. Monroe. But I know better. I feel it in my chest. That sharp, suffocating pain of knowing something is terribly wrong.

"Charlie?" I whisper. I don't want to wake the rest of the house. I stand and quickly step into my dress. The boards beneath my feet creak with each step down the hall.

By the time I reach the kitchen, the scent of woodsmoke and baking bread hits me. Mrs. Monroe stands at the stove, stoking the fire. She glances up, her face pale, her hands trembling as she works. No doubt she's been up for hours, worrying about John.

"Charlie's not here," I say softly, my throat tight, voice catching.

Mrs. Monroe drops the iron spoon she's holding. It clatters to the floor with a sharp clang.

Charlie reminds me so much of my little sister, Nina. They're the same age... and as I think of Nina, a memory rushes in, so vivid it feels like it just happened. We were all gathered in this very house when Aunt Ida told us about this infamous day. About this battle. I remember the way Nina's face fell when she learned that the Monroe family had lost a child in the war.

I was so focused on Eric, I never took a moment to think about the Monroes losing Charlie... maybe I just wouldn't let my mind go to that dark of a place....

"Oh, God!" Mrs. Monroe cries out, her voice echoing through the house.

Within the hour, every able body who hasn't marched off to the hill is scouring the woods, the creeks, the trails into town. Mr. Monroe and the neighbors check the meeting houses, the blacksmith's shop, the stables.

No one says it aloud, but we all feel it in our bones. Charlie has gone to fight.

There's no word of a girl posing as a young man. But then again, who would know? Charlie is stubborn, clever, and brave enough to sneak out in the dark wearing a pair of John's trousers, her hair pinned up and tucked under a cap.

I can't sit still and wait. Knowing Eric and Charlie might die out there claws through me like poison in my veins. With Uncle Arthur's map of the nearby farms folded tightly in my pocket, I ask Charlie's younger brother to saddle the Monroes' gentlest mare, the one I've only ridden a few times while helping with chores. I mount Seonna and steer her toward the stretch of woods that runs between the Monroe and Thomas properties.

If Charlie dies out there, if she never comes back, I don't know how I'll live with myself. I knew this was coming, and I didn't stop her. I just didn't think she would go without me. Charlie is fearless, yes, but she's also reckless, and I was so wrapped up in my own worries and desires that I completely let her down.

The thought of her lying somewhere on that battlefield, hurt or worse, makes my stomach twist into a knot. I keep thinking of Nina, of how devastated I'd be if it were her. How devastated the Monroes will be if Charlie doesn't come home.

A hawk screams above me, circling. The wind blows the scent of gunpowder from the battlefield. The mare's hooves crunch over old leaves and packed dirt. I lean forward in the saddle, eyes scanning for any sign of Charlie. The woods offer no answers.

Then I hear it. Low rumbles that roll like waves through the earth. Cannons have been booming all morning, but now they are followed by the pops and cracks of muskets. That means they've reached the shore. The first assault has begun.

The battle is happening right now, and I'm close enough to feel the ground hum beneath my feet. Part of me wants to ride toward it, to look for her. But I know better. My presence on the battlefield would just be a distraction for Eric, and that's the last thing he needs right now.

Instead, I tug the reins and turn Seonna back toward safety. I pray Charlie is safe and that she is not anywhere near Breed's Hill.

Then, just as I begin to turn, something flickers at the edge of my vision. Red. I freeze and hold my breath.

A British soldier.

Slowly leaning forward, I strain to listen. I hear a rustle then a soft groan. Glancing around, I try to ascertain if there are other Redcoats nearby. I don't know if he's seen me. If I bolt, the noise might draw attention.

I slide off the horse. Quietly, cautiously, I step through the brush. When I am a few feet closer, I can see him clearly now.

He's young. No older than Charlie. His coat is soaked with blood, and one of his legs is twisted beneath him. His face is white as milk, his lips cracked and red. He gasps for air, and when he tries to stand, he falls back to the ground, moaning louder.

Everything in me screams to run, but I don't. He can't hurt me. The poor kid can barely stay conscious.

"Can you get up?" I ask, my voice low but firm.

He blinks. "Hurts…" he whispers, barely audible.

I kneel next to him, surveying the damage. It looks as though he's been shot in the upper thigh. He winces as I tighten my cloth apron around his leg.

"I've had worse," he mutters, his voice thin and shaking.

"You're a terrible liar," I say, glancing up at his pale face. "You're losing blood faster than I can stop it."

"I'm still breathing, aren't I?" He forces a weak smile.

"You're just a boy," I whisper, half to myself.

He hears me anyway. "So are most of the lads out there. They don't care how old we are, not when we've got muskets in our hands."

"What's your name?" I ask.

"Martin," he replies, gasping for air between each word. "I'm from London."

"I'm Hattie from just over that hill," I nod in the direction of the Monroe house. "It's a blessing I found you."

"You don't have to help me, miss. I understand. I am the enemy."

"No," I say quietly. "You don't look like the enemy. You look like someone's son."

I slip his arm over my shoulders, which is awkward and painful for us both. He's heavy, and I'm not strong enough to carry him for long. Finally, with a lot of grimaces and gasps, we get to the mare.

He slumps against her side, and I brace his weight with my hip. I grunt as I haul him up with everything I have. The boy screams in agony.

Once he's in the saddle, I mount up behind him and wrap one arm around his chest to keep him from falling off. He mutters incoherently, most likely due to blood loss, before going limp against me.

Blood soaks through his coat and stains my sleeve. I don't know what I'm doing. He's the enemy. What will the Monroe's say when they see us riding up? They took me in without hesitation. I hope they will be as kind to Martin, even if he is wearing red. He's a bleeding boy, and we can't let him die in the dirt.

I urge Seonna forward, pulse racing, eyes scanning the woods. The trip back to the Monroe house seems to take forever. Looking at the amount of blood he's losing, I pray we reach it in time.

Shifting in the saddle, I try to keep Martin from sliding off. His blood seeps through to the saddle blanket, and I can feel the weakening of his body as he leans heavier against mine. Every step Seonna takes jostles him, causing him to moan.

I don't even know if we're doing the right thing, if saving him will bring more trouble to the Monroes, or if it's even possible to save him. I grit my teeth and press forward. If Charlie can march into battle with a musket, I can manage to bring one wounded kid home.

The trees thin out as we near the Monroe yard. Smoke drifts on the air from far off. By now, Charleston is burning, and I'm riding in the opposite direction of it all. I don't know who I'm trying to save anymore, but I know I can't let this boy die alone.

CHAPTER TWENTY-ONE

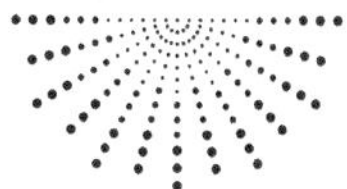

THE HORSE IS SOAKED WITH BLOOD, AND MY ARMS ARE SHAKING FROM the effort of holding Martin upright. His weight is dead against mine. His head droops on my shoulder, breath shallow, barely there. The smell of smoke clings to the breeze, and the sky above the trees is stained the color of rust and ash.

We round the bend, and at last, I see the white slats of the Monroe house through the trees. The sight nearly knocks the breath out of me. As we enter the yard, I call out with what little strength I have left.

"Help! Mrs. Monroe! Help! Please!"

The front door flies open, slamming behind her as she crosses the porch and rushes down the steps.

"Hattie? What the blazes?"

"This boy is hurt bad," I choke out, barely able to speak through the pounding in my head. "He's a British soldier, but he's just a boy."

Mrs. Monroe doesn't hesitate. She takes one look at the limp form draped across my lap and grabs the reins.

"Get down. I'll hold him steady," she says.

I slide down off the horse, legs trembling, and together we ease Martin from the saddle. He moans faintly as we lower him, his eyelids moving but not waking.

Hearing the commotion, Mr. Monroe appears, face grim, sleeves already rolled up. He doesn't ask questions. Between the three of us, we carry the boy into the house and lay him out in a bed in the servant's quarters, a small room just off the kitchen.

I lean against the wall, dizzy. My hands are coated in blood. My dress is soaked in it. The sickly-sour scent turns my stomach.

Mrs. Monroe is already at work, slicing away his pants with practiced efficiency. "Gunshot," she mutters. "This leg's in bad shape. Hattie, get more water from the well. As much as you can carry, and tell everyone you see along the way that we need help. We need to start carrying in water, boiling water, and keep it boiling all day. He's the first, but certainly not the last."

Glad she knows enough about sanitary conditions to boil the water, I bolt out the door to the well, pulling up a bucket, though my muscles scream in protest. The second bucket sloshes over my skirts, but I don't stop. I haul it back inside where Mr. Monroe has set up the kettle on the fire, and the house already smells of scorched linen and blood.

I go back to check on the boy and find that Martin still isn't awake. Mrs. Monroe washes the gash with boiled water, presses strips of clean linen into the wound, and binds his leg with torn sheets. The bleeding slows.

I stand at the doorway, helpless, trying not to cry. "Is he going to die?" I whisper.

Mrs. Monroe doesn't look up. "Not if we can help it. Go sit, child. You're shaking."

But I can't sit.

I pace the kitchen, then the front parlor, then the hall. My eyes stray constantly on the windows. Every pop and crack of musket fire in the distance makes my heart leap into my throat.

Where is Charlie? Where is Eric?

Are they dead already? Is this boy the first sign of how bad it's going to get?

The minutes drag on. I check on Martin. He's still unconscious, but his chest rises and falls. That's something. Mrs. Monroe wraps another bandage around his leg, whispering softly, something like a prayer.

Sick with worry, Mrs. Monroe and I have no appetite for the noonday meal, yet we keep our hands busy in the kitchen, working alongside the household staff to prepare a generous meal for Mr. Monroe, the children, and the others who serve the family. She moves with calm determination. We make extra food for the soldiers who we know will soon come to the Monroe home for help.

It is clear this is not Mrs. Monroe's first time facing hardship. It's as if she's been preparing for this very moment her entire life. I watch in quiet awe as she gives clear, steady instructions, ensuring every pot is filled, every loaf possible is baked, every hand assigned a task. She speaks with certainty, already anticipating that more wounded soldiers will arrive by evening, and she intends to be ready when they do.

Then around dinner time we hear it. Right outside the front door, not a knock, really. More like a thud.

I open the door.

A soldier leans against the frame, one arm dangling uselessly. His coat is torn, and his face is smeared with dirt and sweat. He looks at me with eyes glazed from pain.

"I can't… walk no more."

I catch him just as he falls.

"Mr. Monroe!" I call, struggling under the weight. "We need help!"

They come fast after that, like a dam breaking.

One after another. Some limping. Some carried. One boy is barely conscious, slumped between two others who don't look much better. There are gashes and bullet wounds, broken bones and scorched skin. The porch becomes a triage line. The kitchen fills with groans and prayers. The hallway becomes a bed of blankets and blood.

The Monroes' elegant home transforms before our eyes. The

parlor rug is rolled back, furniture shoved against the walls. We use every chair, every couch, bed, and makeshift table. A few straw mattresses are dragged out from the barn loft and laid on the dining room floor, a soldier lying on each. Sheets are torn. Every towel becomes a compress.

"Boil more water," Mrs. Monroe orders. "We need more clean rags."

I run without thinking. My body moves on instinct now. Pour, carry, bind, repeat. The wounded call out for their mothers, for God, for water. I hear every kind of cry: anger, pain, despair.

Some of them look like men and boys. Others like ghosts.

One man comes in cradling a broken arm. I recognize him from church.. His face is pale, speckled with blood. He doesn't look at me when I ask about Charlie. He only shakes his head.

"I didn't see her."

"Eric Thomas?" I ask, my voice cracking.

"I didn't see him, miss," he murmurs. "It was chaos."

Chaos.

He sinks to the floor. I tie his arm in a makeshift cloth sling and move on. We work until the sun is gone, and then we work by candlelight.

Mrs. Monroe tends wounds and whispers motherly words of comfort. Mr. Monroe doesn't speak much, but he bandages arms, helps set bones the best he can, and carries the dying into the back room where we lay them out in silence.

One British boy, no more than sixteen, dies holding my hand. His name was Elijah. He didn't want to die alone.

I think of my high school students back home in Seattle, and the tears roll down my cheeks, hot and fierce. I bite down hard on my lip, trying to keep from sobbing. There's a mother somewhere who will never see her son walk through the door again. Maybe a sister who'll wait for a letter that never comes. A father who'll bury his grief in silence. My heart breaks for them. For the family that will sit down at a table with an empty chair and feel the weight of it for the rest of their lives.

It's too much. All of it. The blood, the fear, the endless waiting for people I love to come back, if they ever do. I can't stop the tears now, and I don't try to. I just cry, aching for Eric and Charlie and for a boy I never knew, for his family who will never know me. For my parents and my sister and the students I left behind in another century, another life.

Martin stirs again late in the evening. His lips are cracked, and he whispers something I don't understand.

"Martin," I say, brushing sweat from his brow. "You're safe."

He blinks at me, confused. "I... should be dead."

"No," I say firmly. "You're going to live."

He doesn't answer but is able to take a sip of the water I offer him, which is a good sign.

Across the room, another man begins to cough, wet and choking. Mrs. Monroe rushes to his side.

Someone wails from a back room. I lose track of how many we've helped. Of how many we've lost. And in this moment, it doesn't matter what side of the battle they were on. British, colonial, militia, Redcoat, rebel, patriot. None of it matters. Every single one of them deserves to live. They are sons, brothers, husbands, some of them boys not yet old enough to shave. War feels foolish now. Senseless and cruel. Nothing noble, nothing glorious. Just pain, blood, and the endless sound of people crying out for someone who will never come.

At some point, the floor is red. The smell of blood, sweat, and fear clings to everything. My hands shake when I try to pour water. My feet ache. But I keep going.

We all do. There's no other choice.

"More bandages," I say, tearing a pillowcase. "I'll soak it."

Mrs. Monroe nods but says nothing. Her face is set like stone. I know she's thinking about John and Charlie, too. Her daughter disguised in her son's clothes. Two of her children on that hill, maybe bleeding. Maybe worse.

"Have you heard anything?" I ask, my voice low.

She shakes her head once. "No word."

The Monroe house becomes a battlefield of its own. A quieter one, but no less brutal. Men moan in fever dreams. Some beg to go home. Some scream. One loses his mind entirely, lashing out until Mr. Monroe pins him down and doses him with some of the little laudanum we have left.

Through it all, I keep checking the windows. Waiting. Any shadow on the road could be Eric. Any figure in the woods could be Charlie.

By midnight, we have more than twenty men lying on the floor, in corners, and across every surface. We've run out of clean rags. My arms feel like they'll fall off. Still, I keep moving.

I'm afraid if I stop, I'll collapse. Or worse, I'll start to imagine that Charlie's already gone.

That Eric won't come back.

That the future I long for with Eric is gone with the smoke rising from Bunker Hill.

But for now, I work. I boil water. I press a cloth to a wound. I hold another boy's hand.

I whisper promises I can't keep.

CHAPTER TWENTY-TWO

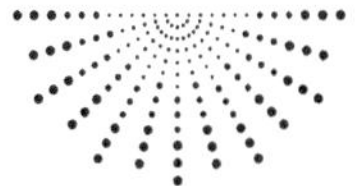

Eric

"Fix bayonets!"

The order rips through the chaos, louder than the screaming and sharper than the crack of musket fire. Men around me scramble to obey. I drop to one knee, shaking fingers sliding my own bayonet onto the end of the musket. The steel clicks into place. My last round is gone.

All around us, the line is falling quiet with focus and anticipation. We're out of ammunition, and now we must look our enemies in the eye.

The British still have powder, and their volleys are relentless. From across the smoke, we hear the sharp rhythm of their organized fire.

A man ten paces to my right falls backward, a hole in his throat. Another clutches his stomach and screams.

Still, no orders to retreat.

I grit my teeth and stand, heart hammering, sweat stinging my eyes. Smoke curls low and thick, choking the hillside, making everything dim and ghostly. My muscles are tight, breath ragged. Some-where beyond this curtain of gunpowder and blood, the Redcoats are advancing again.

The third assault, just as Hattie predicted.

Their boots pound the earth. The ground seems to tremble beneath them.

"We can't hold this," I mutter.

Colin is beside me, breathing hard. "We hold till we're told otherwise."

"We won't be told anything if we're all dead," I snap.

"They're coming!" John yells.

Figures emerge from the haze. Bright red. Their line is tighter this time. They're yelling, battle cries and curses, as they charge.

"Hold!" someone shouts.

We don't. We can't. We are outnumbered.

A man staggers ahead of me, shrieking in agony, swinging his empty musket like a club. Another lifts a hatchet. Out of the corner of my eye, I see Levi lower his stance, bracing for impact. John, too. His jaw is set, grip firm.

Then the two sides collide in our part of the line. Bayonet versus bayonet. Steel slamming into bone. Musket stocks crashing against skulls.

I parry a thrust and bash the British soldier's face with the butt of my gun. He goes down, screaming, and I stab him in the chest with my bayonet. I don't stop to look. There's no time.

It's carnage. Raw and personal. I dodge a lunge, duck under a swing, shove my bayonet into a man's shoulder and hear him howl.

A Redcoat falls nearby at the hand of Levi, but two more are already closing in. I push through to help, fighting one off while Colin stabs the other in the back with his bayonet.

"Fall back!" I shout. "We need to fall back! Now!"

"We haven't gotten the order!" Colin shouts back.

"There may not be anyone left to give it!" I yell.

"We're supposed to hold!" Levi adds, eyes scanning for another threat.

John shakes his head, digging in. "We're not leaving this line. Not until we're told."

"We'll die here!" I yell.

"I'd rather die than run," John snaps.

In the midst of our argument, a gunshot cracks the air. I hear it before I see it. Then I see him stumble. John's eyes gloss over, and he drops his musket. His mouth falls open in shock just before he crumples.

"No! John!" I'm already moving.

I catch him before he hits the ground completely. Colin and Levi dive in to help, firing panicked looks over their shoulders.

The British are surging forward, but their formation is breaking. They're momentarily confused. We have only seconds.

"Help me lift him!" I shout, voice ragged.

Colin grabs his legs, Levi his arms. We pick him up and run.

Musket balls zip past us, buzzing like hornets. One hits a tree just ahead, and bark explodes in my face. We can't stop running.

The forest swallows us, and my lungs burn. We run deeper until the sounds of battle fade into the background like thunder after a storm.

We find cover behind a mossy rock shelf and lay John down. His chest is soaked red. The wound is high, just beneath the collarbone, and the blood is thick and bubbling.

Levi rips cloth from his sleeve and presses it to the wound.

John groans.

"Stay with us," I whisper, kneeling beside him. "You're going to be fine. You're going to make it home. We'll get you home."

He blinks slowly and tries to respond, but blood spills from his lips.

Colin leans in, brushing sweat from our friend's forehead. "We are here, John. We've got you."

John struggles to breathe, and I hear blood gurgling in his throat.

And then he's gone.

I freeze. The world seems to drop out from under me.

Colin shakes him. "John? John!"

Nothing.

Levi pulls back, breath shaky. "No. No, come on—"

"He's gone," I whisper.

I press my hand to John's chest. It doesn't rise.

We sit there in stunned silence, the three of us, huddled around the body of my best friend from as far back as I can remember. He was just here. We were just fighting alongside one another. He was just arguing with me….

I bow my head, rage crawling up my throat. Not at him. Not even at the Redcoats. At the damn senselessness of it.

I clench my jaw. "We should've left sooner."

"We couldn't," Colin mutters. "There is no honor in an early retreat. He fought well. He fought courageously."

"No one was giving orders anymore," I snap. "The line was breaking. I should've pulled us back. I should've made him—"

Levi puts a hand on my shoulder. "We didn't listen to you, brother. You tried."

"Not hard enough."

We take cover in the forest until dusk. The sounds of war fade into bird calls and wind. When it's finally safe, we lift John again, gently this time.

Colin wraps his arms around John's legs, Levi supports his shoulders, and I steady the middle, one hand across his back, the other beneath the curve of his ribs, where the blood is still warm. His clothes are soaked through.

The overwhelming smell of iron, sweat and the smoke of the battlefield follows us. We walk in silence, the three of us navigating the uneven forest path, our boots crunching over twigs and damp leaves. The woods are hushed now, as if even nature understands what we've lost.

No one says a word for a long while. I know where we're headed. We all do. We stop often and lower our friend's body so we can rest a moment.

When the trees begin to part, and I glimpse the slope of our family's land in the distance, a weight is lifted from my shoulders. The familiar fields are bathed in moonlight, and it's so comforting, it's cruel because everything looks the same as it did when we left–except now, John's gone. Now, John can't see it, too.

The back door creaks open before we even reach the porch. Mother stands in the doorway, dish towel in her hands. She looks at the three of us boys, covered in blood, carrying John, and her face is a mixture of hope and despair. She doesn't scream. Doesn't cry. Just steps back and opens the door wider.

"Bring him in," she says quietly.

Father meets us in the parlor, eyes rimmed red. He takes one look and moves the table aside so we can lay John on the rug. Levi finds a spare quilt and drapes it over him, up to his shoulders. Colin pulls leaves and dirt from John's hair.

Mother kneels beside my friend. "He was always so kind," she murmurs. "Even when he was a little boy. Always taking care of others before himself."

I look away, my throat tight. Pain rushes through my veins.

Mother rises and kisses each of her sons on the forehead, whispering a prayer of thanks to God for bringing us home.

"I'll boil water," Mother says. "I'll clean him up."

"We should do it," I tell her, forcing my voice steady. "He was our brother, even if not by blood."

Father nods. "Praise be to God for bringing my sons back to me. I'll see to the horses and wagon. You'll need them in the morning," he says with tears in his eyes.

The words hit like a punch to the gut. Of course. We have to tell them. John's parents. His younger siblings. They'll be expecting him home. I imagine them watching the road, scanning the faces of every passing rider, smiling whenever they think they see someone famil-iar–frowning when they realize they don't.

I don't know how we're supposed to tell them they will never see John again.

The fire crackles low as Colin, Levi, and I clean John's face and hands. The blood on his chest has already begun to dry and darken, and the bullet wound has stopped leaking, though that only makes it worse. There's a finality to it.

Colin and Levi move quietly, hands steady. We've dressed wounds before, tended to the wounded and dying at Lexington and Concord, but this is different. This isn't healing. This is saying goodbye. And this is John.

I help Mother fold his hands over his chest and tuck the quilt tighter around him. I stare at his face for a long time, never wanting to forget him.

He looks younger now. Still. Peaceful.

After we prepare his body, I step outside to breathe. The night air is cool on my face, the sky deep blue and dotted with stars. I rest my hand on the porch railing and let my weight settle into it.

I should feel relief that we made it home alive. That Levi and Colin are safe. That I'll see Mother and Father in the morning. That there's food and shelter and a bed that doesn't reek of mud and death.

And I should be so very grateful for Hattie.

But now John's gone.

I stare at the sky and feel the first prick of tears behind my eyes. I won't cry. Not yet.

Behind me, the door creaks again. Colin steps out, arms crossed, Levi on his heels.

"What do we even say?" Levi finally asks.

I rub my hands over my face. "We tell them the truth. That he fought bravely. That he refused to retreat early. That he didn't flinch. That he saved lives."

"We tell them he didn't suffer," Colin adds.

Levi nods solemnly. "Right."

As we enter the house to go to sleep for what's left of the night, my heart aches.

I should be thinking about Hattie. About kissing her again. About telling her I'm safe. But every time I close my eyes, all I see is John's mouth falling open. His musket slipping from his hands. Blood everywhere.

It'll be a long time before I see anything else.

CHAPTER TWENTY-THREE

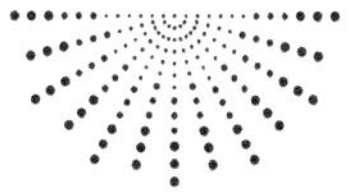

Hattie

The sun hasn't dared rise yet, but the eastern sky begins to erupt in shades of pink and orange. The porch boards creak beneath me as I shift my weight, stiff from where I sit, half-leaning, half-upright, against the rail. My dress is bunched under me, my arms crossed over my chest, the warmth of the last soldier I tended lingering. Someone moans nearby. Another man coughs. Beyond that sits the silence, thick and awful, the kind that only follows cannon fire and screams.

Half sleeping, half watching for any sign of Charlie, Eric, or a familiar face in the fog, I blink hard, trying to keep my eyes open, but sleep pulls at me like the tide. My hands are stained with blood, some dried, some fresh, and I've long since stopped noticing the iron smell of it. Now, the air is beginning to reek of decomposing bodies.

I've been awake for... I don't even know how long. Since I first heard the thunder of the cannons yesterday at dawn.

It's Sunday morning now, that much I know. But I can't bear to sit with what that means. If it's morning, then the battle is over. And if the battle is over, then Eric is already gone.

My head droops forward. Just for a minute, I tell myself. Just long enough to rest my eyes—

"Hattie. Hattie! Wake up—please—wake up!"

Hands shake me, gently at first, then more urgently. I jolt, eyes flying open to find a figure crouched in front of me, gripping my shoulders. It's a boy wearing a rough coat, pants torn at the knees, face shadowed by the brim of a tricorn hat.

Disoriented, I scramble backward on the porch, hands ready to shove him away until I catch a glimpse of the eyes. They're worried and familiar.

"Charlie?" The word is a croak.

She pulls off the hat.

It *is* Charlie!

I lunge forward and throw my arms around her, clutching her tight. Her rifle bumps my shoulder, and she stumbles slightly beneath the force of my hug, but she doesn't let go, and neither do I.

"You're alive," I whisper, not even realizing the tears had started until one splashes onto her cheek. "Oh, Charlie, you're alive."

"I made it back," she says, voice trembling against my ear. "I'm all right, Hattie."

I pull away just enough to look at her. There's a smear of soot across her forehead, a tear in her coat, and a line of dried blood under her chin, but she's standing, breathing, speaking. She's whole.

"You absolutely terrified us!"

"I know," she says, weakly.

"What in God's name were you thinking?"

"You inspired me," she explains.

"I what?"

"The day we met," she says, stepping back. "You showed up in men's trousers. You speak of how different women's lives are in the future. I wanted to be brave like that. Like you. I wanted to help change this country for the better. To make a contribution to the women of the future."

Emotion rises sharp and sudden in my chest. I swallow hard and reach for her again. "Thank you for your service, Private Monroe," I say, the words catching on the lump in my throat.

Inside the house, Mrs. Monroe yells, "Charlie?"

Seconds later, she bursts through the door and freezes at the sight of Charlie, dressed in men's clothes, her hair tucked haphazardly under her cap. Then she throws her arms around her daughter and sobs.

Everyone's awake by now, those who aren't wounded beyond sense, anyway. A few heads lift. Someone calls out in a broken voice, "She's back!" And a ripple of relief spreads through the crowd gathered on the porch and lawn. It seems everyone was keeping an eye out for Charlie.

Mr. Monroe comes outside next. He looks at Charlie, looks at the sky, and falls to his knees to pray. I have no doubt he is thanking God for bringing his Charlotte home.

While all the children scold Charlie and kiss her cheeks. I can't help but laugh from a place of relief, stepping back to let them have her.

My hands are still stained, my sleeves are crusted, my head spins, and I think I might pass out, but Charlie is home, and right now that is something to be joyful about.

By mid-morning, the Monroes' yard is a field hospital in all but name. Blankets are laid out on the grass. Buckets of water are rushed back and forth. Loaves of bread disappear almost as fast as they're sliced. Mrs. Monroe and the children pass out food and try to make the soldiers comfortable.

Charlie and I move among the wounded, changing bandages, and offering water. Neither of us say much; we just work. She asked if John had returned yet as soon as everyone let go of her, but no one had the heart to answer aloud. Everyone simply shook their heads.

I want to ask her about the battle, ask her if she saw Eric, but I don't dare. If she saw him, she would tell me.

I know Eric isn't coming home.

I tie a fresh bandage around a young soldier's arm. He thanks me, eyes tired and hollow. I stand and wipe my hands on my apron then turn to see three horses kicking up dust on the road.

My heart stops.

The rider and wagon come into view, and for one terrible moment I can't breathe. Then I recognize them—Colin, Levi, and—

Eric.

I run.

I forget everything. I forget the wounded, the blood on my hands and face, the ache in my spine. I lift my skirt and *run*. Eric sees me and kicks his horse faster, swinging off the saddle before the animal has even stopped. We meet halfway between the yard and the road.

He catches me in his arms and lifts me off the ground. I throw my arms around his neck, and bury my face in his shoulder. I don't care who sees. I don't care what they think. I feel so light.

He's *alive*.

He smells like gunpowder, horses, leather, and smoke. His hair is damp with sweat. There's worry in his eyes, and his coat is torn, but he holds me so tightly, and I never want him to let go.

"I thought—" I start.

"I know," he says. His voice is hoarse.

"I didn't know if—"

"I'm here." He pulls back just enough to look at me. "You're safe. I'm safe."

"John?" I ask, dread rising up my throat.

His eyes darken. "Please," he says, his voice rough, "let us just have this brief moment."

I nod and hold him.

Colin and Levi drive a covered wagon, both looking weary. Charlie rushes to meet them, and Colin startles, staring at her in disbelief. Then he jumps down and grabs her in a bear hug. Levi hops off the wagon, ruffles her hair, and mutters something I can't hear, but the smile on his face says everything.

Eric finally lets me go but doesn't release my hand. His fingers are rough and warm against mine. "You've been helping the wounded all night?" he asks, glancing around at the rows of injured men.

I nod. "They kept coming. Some on foot. Some carried. A few... didn't make it."

He squeezes my hand tighter.

"I found a British soldier in the woods yesterday while I was looking for Charlie," I tell him, my voice low. "A young boy... Martin.... I brought him here."

Eric raises his eyebrows, "You saved his life?"

"I just couldn't let him die alone."

CHAPTER TWENTY-FOUR

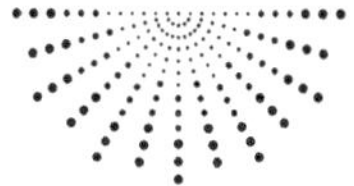

Eric

I want to hold her forever.

Hattie buries her face in my chest, arms locked around me like she's afraid I'll vanish again. And part of me wants to vanish, to be invisible, so that I don't have to speak the words that will break hearts.

But the moment doesn't last—

"No…."

The word is barely a whisper, riding on a breath of disbelief. Mrs. Monroe is standing on her porch, her apron stained rusty blood red. Her hands are full of rags and bandages. Her voice grows louder as she steps forward, a kind of dread rising like smoke from a fire. She drops the linens, takes off running, and by the time she reaches me, she is screaming.

"No! No! No! No!"

Each word is a blow…. By the last one, she has nothing left and submits to the pain of reality.

Hattie steps aside to give us space. Mrs. Monroe beats my chest with her fists. Not hard enough to hurt. She is just trying to fight grief away, and I can't blame her. Her sobs fill the air around us. I don't try to stop her. I only wrap my arms around her and let her grieve the way she needs to, pressing her face to my shoulder like I can absorb the weight of her loss.

The realization hits Charlie, who collapses right where she stands, knees in the dirt, a soundless gasp leaving her mouth before she doubles over and covers her face. Hattie darts to her side and folds her into her arms, whispering something I can't hear. Her eyes are on me, though, red and full of sorrow.

Mr. Monroe doesn't say a word. He just lowers his head, shoulders shaking under the weight of grief. Stepping down off the porch, he comes to collect his wife.

Mrs. Monroe has gone limp in my arms, her sobs still coming in waves. I lift her off the ground. Colin and I help carry her inside. The Monroes' home usually smells like wood smoke, bread, and herbs, but today the scent of blood is overwhelming.

We help Mrs. Monroe to her bedroom and into the bed. Hattie appears at the doorway, still holding Charlie, who runs over to the bed and lies next to her mother. The two of them weep, trying to console one another. Mr. Monroe steps into the room, and Hattie and I give them their privacy. He closes the door behind us, but we can hear the wailing from the other side.

Hattie and I walk out onto the porch. Her eyes glisten with unshed tears, and when she looks at me, she steps forward. I pull her into my arms again. This time, we don't speak for a long while.

My brothers and I take over for the Monroes helping Hattie care for the wounded all day. We check on them often and make sure they all drink water and get something for dinner. The children have been told of their brother's death and their tearful, little faces pull at the strings of my heart.

When the sky begins to darken, and the wounded men who live nearby begin to return to their own homes, the others to their cots, Hattie takes my hand.

"Will you tell me what happened?" she asks quietly. "Please?"

I nod, escorting her to the edge of the field where the grass is long and wild, hiding us from the view of the house. We sit down on a patch of soft earth, the tall blades bending around us like a curtain. I take Hattie's hand in mine and inhale deeply.

"I still hear the bayonets striking bone. Still smell the powder, mud, and blood. And in the middle of it, John, fighting like hell. We held them off twice. They came up the hill, and we drove them back. The third time we were out of powder. We had almost nothing. Our captain told us to use our bayonets, rocks, our fists, anything we had left. It was utter chaos. Smoke so thick you could barely see your hand in front of your face. And then they broke through."

Hattie's fingers tighten around mine.

"I stuck close to my brothers. And John." My voice falters. "He was... God, he was brave. He didn't want to quit. We were out of ammunition, and he didn't want to give up, no matter how much I tried to convince him to retreat with me before we were given that command."

"You tried to save them? And yourself? You took what I said to heart? For me?" she asks.

"I would do anything for you. And Hattie, you were right. You were right about everything. I still don't know how, but you were." I stroke her cheek.

She says nothing, but she's biting her bottom lip, which makes me think she's considering saying something.

I continue before I lose the ability to do so. "Just as we were turning to run, he got shot. Up by his collar bone. It didn't take him long to die." I can barely force the words out.

"I'm so sorry," she whispers.

We lie side by side in the field for hours, wisps of battle smoke clinging to the air like a veil, blurring the stars above us. Hattie's red curls fan out across the grass, catching what little light filters through. Her hand is in mine, warm and still. We're too tired to speak, and that's just as well. Lying here beside her is enough.

Somewhere in the distance, a whippoorwill cries, and for a second, the world doesn't feel like it's ending. I study her profile in the dim light, how her lashes rest against her cheek, the curve of her mouth, the smudge of wood stove ash still clinging to her jaw. She's been through hell, too, and she's still here. Still kind, beautiful Hattie.

For the first time in days, I feel my breathing settle. There's still blood under my nails, and my shoulder aches from carrying more weight than one man should. But Hattie's sweet spirit is the one breath of innocence his war hasn't ruined. Everything else feels worn thin or half-broken, but she's still light, soft and steady, like a wild-flower growing where no one thought life could take root.

"Hattie?" I break the silence, leaning up on my elbow. "I don't know what tomorrow will look like. Not anymore. Not after what we saw. But I do know this...."

She sits up then, eyes locked on mine, and I almost don't say it. The words gather, but fear nearly stops them. Not of her answer, but of daring to want something this good in a world that keeps stealing all that's good away. What if saying it out loud makes it easier to lose? But then she shifts closer, her hand brushing mine again, and that tiny touch is enough to remind me that if I don't ask, I'll regret it forever.

"I don't want to wait until the war is over. That might never come. This land is charged with friction, and there have been battles here for years. It won't be easy, but I want to build whatever comes next with you. I want to wake up beside you when the worst has passed, and even when it hasn't. I want you beside me in whatever version of the future we are destined for. Will you marry me?"

She doesn't cry. She doesn't gasp. She just leans in, presses her forehead to mine, and lets the silence answer first.

"Yes," she says, soft but certain.

I close my eyes and kiss her deeply. What I feel is not exactly relief but something deeper, and we are so overcome with grief, it feels like the earth could swallow us whole. But we have each other.

Tomorrow, we'll help the Monroes properly bury their son, my greatest friend and the bravest man I ever knew.

Tonight, there are beginnings of something that might just be strong enough to survive whatever comes next.

CHAPTER TWENTY-FIVE

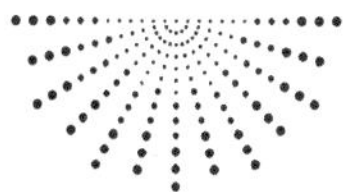

THREE WEEKS LATER...
Hattie

I SIT ALONE IN A ROCKING CHAIR ON THE MONROES' PORCH, WHICH seems to creak in rhythm with the cicadas. My dress is stained with blue juice and dirt. Charlie and I spent all afternoon picking blueberries, and now she and the children are in the kitchen washing them. The sun hangs low, slipping toward the hills like it's trying to escape. How I envy it.

A thousand memories from home drift through my mind like the songs I heard on the radio as a kid. Familiar, comforting, and laced with a kind of warmth a person doesn't recognize until it's gone. My sister laughing at my dad's cheesy jokes. My mom calling every time she got a good deal at a clearance sale. Pizza. Oh, how I long for a big slice of pepperoni pizza with extra cheese. And my students, of course....

My family doesn't know where I am. They must think I'm dead. I miss them so much, it's a physical ache. A hollow pain that never goes away, no matter how many days pass. No matter how deeply I've fallen in love with this world and with Eric, I don't belong here.

In 1775, I'm a curiosity at best. At worst, a danger to myself and others–like Charlie. Here, women's voices are hushed, their futures sewn into marriage and childbirth. It's a beautiful world in many ways, but not mine. It's not for me. I will slip up, be too opinionated for this era. The first time I see the atrocities and inhumanities that this century has been subjected to, I will not bite my tongue. I'll start the abolitionist movement and the suffrage movement on the same day and be burned at the stake while people call me a witch....

I can't teach here, publish easily, or walk alone without suspicion. I left behind a career I worked hard for, friends I chose, a life I built on my own terms. And I miss my wonderful family.

Eric has made me feel strong, loved, and seen, but loving him doesn't erase everything else I am.

And that's the truth I've been choking on. The reason I've kept my secret buried beneath every kiss, every promise. Once I say it out loud, everything changes.

For the past three weeks, I've lived with the guilt of accepting his proposal, not because I don't love him, but because I do, with every piece of me. And still, I can't stay. Loving him doesn't rewrite who I am or where I belong.

The note is folded in my pocket. Not that it says much, just a scrawl of words I forced myself to write this morning in case I start to stammer and lose my train of thought.

I'm not from here. I've lied to you. But I swear, I never meant to hurt you.

It sounds ridiculous on paper. Who would believe it? That I fell through time. That I don't belong in this century.

But the weight of the truth is crushing me now. I can't carry it any longer. Not when Eric looks at me like I'm his whole world. Not when I know what I'm planning to do tonight. I have to tell him before I disappear. Before I dive back into that well and pray it still holds the same strange magic that brought me here.

I press my palms to my eyes. How do you say goodbye to the

person who made you believe you could belong, even in the wrong century?

How do you tell the man you love that you're leaving, not because he isn't enough, but because everything else is?

I rise slowly, shame curling tightly around my chest. I've known since the moment he asked me to marry him that I couldn't stay. But he had just lost his best friend. How could I break his heart again, right then? So I said yes, not out of dishonesty, but out of love. I couldn't bear to add another wound.

Tonight, at midnight, I'll try the well again. But first, I have to tell Eric the truth.

Walking into the kitchen, I tell Charlie that I'm going to see Eric at the cottage and will return shortly.

The sun is dipping below the horizon when I find him. He's behind his cabin splitting wood. The rhythmic crack of the axe is sharp and deliberate. I stand in the shadows for a moment, watching him. His shirt is damp with sweat, dark hair clinging to his brow, jaw clenched with every swing. He is so ruggedly handsome.

I could turn around. Walk away. Leave the note and spare myself the goodbye.

But that would be worse. That would make me a ghost in his life instead of the woman who loved him wholly, if too briefly.

He senses me before I speak. The axe stops mid-swing, and he looks over his shoulder.

"Hattie?"

I step closer. "Can we talk?"

He studies me for a second, then nods, setting the axe aside. He wipes his hands on a cloth and follows me. Neither of us speak at first. I listen to our footsteps in the dirt, the rustle of wind through dry summer leaves, the pounding of my heart.

"I've been thinking about John," Eric says as we sit in the chairs on the cottage porch. His voice is low. "About the way he looked when he died. About how I couldn't stop it."

I touch his arm gently. "Eric, it wasn't your fault."

His expression doesn't change, but he holds my hand. "He died believing in this cause. In freedom. That has to mean something."

"It does," I say. "He was brave. You all were."

"I still think I see him sometimes," Eric admits. "Out of the corner of my eye. I turn, and he's not there, of course." He shakes his head.

"I'm listening," I whisper.

He turns to me fully. "You always do. I've never met anyone like you, Hattie."

Now. Say it.

"I haven't been honest with you," I blurt out.

Eric frowns. "What do you mean?"

"I've told you pieces. But not the whole story."

He waits.

"About where I'm from," I say. "I'm not from the colonies at all."

A pause. "Where is Seattle then?"

I look him in the eye. "I'm from the year 2025."

He stares at me. Blinks. Then laughs, a startled, incredulous sound.

"I'm serious." My voice cracks. "I fell through time. I fell through your well in the year 2025, and when Charlie pulled me out, it was June 1775. That's why I asked you to put a ladder in your well. In case I gain the courage to jump back in and it doesn't work, I'll be able to climb back out. Or if it does work, I can climb out in the future."

His smile falters, and all the color drains from his face. "You're not jesting," Eric finally says.

I shake my head.

"Why… why would you say this now?" he asks, stunned.

"Because I'm leaving tonight. I'm going back. Or at least I'm going to try. Tonight. The way I came."

Silence stretches between us. I can hear the wind in the grass and the wild rush of my own pulse.

"You're leaving?" he repeats.

"Yes."

His voice hardens. "Why?"

"I have a life there. A family. A career. Friends I've known since childhood. People who are probably worried sick."

Eric's hands curl into fists. "And what about here? What about us? I love you, Hattie."

My throat tightens. "That's why I stayed. I couldn't go, not while you were grieving. Not without saying goodbye. But Eric… I was never meant to be here."

"I asked you to marry me," he pleads, voice quivering. "You said yes! I disagree. I think we *were* meant to be together, and that's why you *are* here."

"I said yes because I love you. And I meant it. I still mean it."

He's breathing hard now, chest rising and falling fast. "You said the colonists win. That we survive this war. That we build something better. We can build a life and a family here."

Tears spill down my cheeks. "I have a life. I have a family. I'm so sorry."

He turns away, shoulders tense, staring out at the trees in silence. When he finally speaks, his voice is low but steady. "You're from the future…?"

"Yes." He seems to believe me.

"What's it like?"

The question catches me off guard.

"It's different," I say. "Beautiful and amazing, but much louder and faster. Women can vote, work wherever we like, and we can speak our minds without fear. I'm a teacher. I work with children, teaching them to read and write, in a place called Seattle, Washington, all the way across the country from here. I have students who count on me. I earn my own money. I don't have to be someone's wife just to survive."

Eric's brow furrows, and for a moment, some of the heaviness in his expression lifts. "Seattle, Washington," he repeats slowly, stumbling on the words like they're foreign. Then his eyes flick to mine, curious despite everything. "Is it named after General Washington? Our General Washington?"

"Yes, it is. George Washington became the first president of the United States. The capital of the country is called Washington, D.C., and is named after him, too. He's not a king, though. Instead, he's an elected leader, chosen by the people. It's a very different kind of government, one where power doesn't belong to a single ruler, but to the people themselves. There have been forty-seven presidents by the year 2025."

Eric blinks, clearly surprised, a spark of something hopeful lighting his eyes. "A president," he repeats. Then his face softens, and a slow smile breaks through the shadows. "You know, I've always thought women should be allowed to vote. They do just as much, if not more, of the work around here. They've helped build this country just as much as any man."

I giggle despite the situation. "I agree."

After a long pause, he says, "I could come with you."

I blink. "What?"

"I'll jump into the well. I'll leave everything. If it works for you, maybe it'll work for me, too."

I grab his hands, desperate and terrified. "Eric, no. You have a mother and a father. Brothers and sisters. A war to fight. A cause you believe in. I can't ask you to give that up."

"I'd give anything up for you."

"No," I say. "You *think* you would. But the world I come from isn't easy either. And if it doesn't work? What if we get lost somewhere in between?"

"I'd rather be lost with you than here without you."

We both fall silent. The sky deepens from lavender to indigo, and my palms begin to sweat as I realize I have mere hours left to say my goodbyes.

"I love you," I whisper. "More than I thought possible."

"Then stay."

"I can't. I don't belong here. I'm not made for this century."

He steps forward, cups my face in his hands. "We're made for each other."

Our kiss is slow, trembling. It tastes like a bittersweet memory already fading.

When he pulls back, his voice is hoarse. "When?"

"Midnight."

CHAPTER TWENTY-SIX

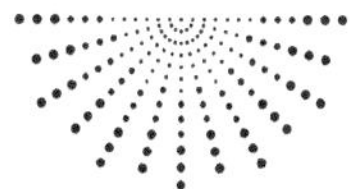

Hattie

THE MOON IS A SILVER COIN DANGLING IN THE NIGHT SKY, CASTING A
pale shimmer over the cottage. I stand next to Eric's stone well, heart
pounding, hands shaking. My jeans and T-shirt feel strange against
my skin after so many weeks in heavy linen dresses.

I can still feel Eric's kiss on my lips, the way his hands cupped my
face like I was something fragile and precious. We hadn't said
goodbye exactly. Neither of us could bear the word, but I'd kissed him
one last time beneath the oak, trying to memorize the taste of him,
the weight of his body against mine. Now, with possibly only seconds
left in this time, I already miss him so much I feel hollow.

I'm surprised Eric didn't show up and try to stop me. He must not
have wanted to watch me leave....

Behind me, Charlie shifts from foot to foot, her arms wrapped
tightly around herself. She looks like she's trying not to cry.

"It's really time then?" she asks, her voice barely above a whisper.

I nod, trying to keep my composure. I've already cried too much tonight, and I don't trust myself not to fall apart again. "If this doesn't work…." I trail off.

"I'll be right here." Charlie stands in front of me and takes my hands. "If you come back up, I'll help you out. I swear."

She's taller than I am and much stronger from years of hard work. Her face shines in the moonlight. I play with the tear in her sleeve from when we helped Martin build a fence earlier this week.

Martin, the soldier boy, decided to stay at the Monroes as a field hand, at least through the summer, maybe longer. His wound has mostly healed, though he still limps a little. I think he needs this place, needs the quiet and the kindness the Monroes have shown him. He said as much to me yesterday when we hauled water together. "Not much left for me back in London," he'd said with a shrug. "Maybe I'll plant something and see if it grows."

I smiled and told him he came to the right place. And now I'm leaving it behind.

"I'm scared," I whisper.

Charlie tightens her grip. "Me, too."

We stand in silence for a few more moments. The cicadas hum. I glance at the well, dark and still, and feel doubt tying a knot deep in my chest. What if it doesn't work? What if I just land at the bottom and break my neck?

"You'll tell them goodbye for me?" I ask.

Charlie sniffles. "Every one of them."

I throw my arms around her. She holds me tightly, the way only a best friend can.

"Go," she whispers in my ear. "Before I drag you back into the house."

I let go, step back, and take one final breath. "I love you."

"I love you, too."

Then I turn, swing one leg over the stone edge, and before I can think too hard, I jump.

Cold water slams into me, wrapping around my body like a fist. I try to scream, but only bubbles escape. The darkness is absolute. No shimmer of moonlight, no trace of the world I just left. Panic surges up inside me.

I'm drowning!

I start to swim toward the surface, desperate against the pull of the current, or maybe just gravity.

My lungs burn, begging for air, but I keep kicking, forcing myself upward through the suffocating dark. Just when I think I won't make it, my head breaks the surface, and I suck in a ragged breath, air flooding my chest like fire.

After I catch my breath, I fumble along the slick sandstone wall, my hands slipping until I find my escape route built right into the wall. Relief crashes over me. Eric built the ladder, just like I asked.

My fingers grip the sides of the stone wall with all my strength. One step after the other, I climb. My wet clothes cling to me, heavy and dripping, but I don't stop. I'm shaking by the time I haul myself over the top and onto the soft grass of the cottage yard.

I lie on my back for a moment, gasping, staring up at the stars. Everything feels different, and my body hurts in a hundred places.

I sit up slowly. Right beside the well lies my phone, dry, whole, and still glowing faintly. I reach for it with trembling fingers. The screen lights up, bright and familiar.

June 10, 2025. 12:04 AM.

I let out a breath. I made it. And I'm right back at the time that I left.

For a terrifying moment, I think maybe I imagined everything. Eric, Charlie, the Monroes, the Battle of Bunker Hill. But the ache in my heart says otherwise, the invisible weight of goodbye still pressing on my shoulders. Tears spill down my cheeks, silent and warm. I'm both happy and heartbroken to be home.

I move through the trees in the direction of the Monroe estate, the soles of my wet shoes whispering against the undergrowth. The woods feel different now, quieter, emptier. In 1775, this forest was alive with birdsong and woodsmoke, the snap of kindling underfoot, the rustle of skirts and boots and boys chasing each other through the leaves. Now, the trees are taller, and the air smells like pollutants and "progress," not hearth fires and bread rising in window sills. For a moment, I swear I hear the faint laughter of the Monroe children echoing through the trees, light and breathless.

The house is dark and quiet when I slip inside. I leave my wet socks and shoes at the back door and pad upstairs. The scent of laundry detergent and lemon cleaner hits me like a punch to the gut, so ordinary, so achingly modern.

I open the bathroom door, flick the light on, and stare at my reflection. I look like a ghost or maybe a zombie.

My hair is plastered to my head, mud is smeared across my cheek, and my eyes are wide and haunted. I turn the water on hot and strip out of my clothes. The shower stings at first, then soothes, washing away the grime of two centuries.

I lean my forehead against the tile and close my eyes. Images flicker behind my lids. Eric's face. Charlie's grin. The Monroes gathered around their table, hands clasped in prayer.

I let the water run until it turns cool, the steam curling around me. I'd almost forgotten how luxurious indoor plumbing really is.

Afterward, I dress in dry pajamas and tiptoe into the bedroom I share with my sister. Nina stirs when I slip under the covers.

"Hattie?" she mumbles sleepily.

"Yeah," I whisper, curling up beside her. "I'm here now."

She drapes an arm over my waist and falls back to sleep.

I lie there, listening to the soft tick of the clock and the gentle hum of electricity in the walls.

The modern world feels strange and much too loud. But I'll adjust.

Still, my heart aches. I miss him already. I fall asleep, reaching for images of him.

The next morning, I wake to the smell of coffee and bacon. The sun is streaming in the window, warm and golden, and for a minute, I pretend it's just a normal summer day.

Then it all comes rushing back.

I sit up slowly, rubbing my eyes. Nina is gone from the bed, probably downstairs eating breakfast.

I press my palm to the mattress, grounding myself. I'm really here. I made it back. It's not a dream. I traveled through time and returned.

After getting dressed and ready for the day, I head downstairs, my heart thudding. Part of me wonders if anyone will notice something's different, since no time passed here at all while I spent a month living in 1775.

The moment I see her, leaning on the kitchen counter in her robe, hair still damp from the shower, I freeze. My mom.

My throat tightens as a rush of emotion barrels through me: relief, disbelief, love. She smiles like she always does, and says, "Morning, honey," as if I haven't been gone a lifetime. I want to fling my arms around her and sob into her shoulder. I want to tell her everything. How I could have died. How I fell in love. How I miss people she's never met….

But I just nod, swallowing hard. "Morning," I manage, voice shaking. And that single word contains everything I can't yet say.

"There you are," Nina says, her voice light. "You were out cold."

I nod. "Sorry. I was… just… exhausted."

She smiles. "You okay?"

I hesitate. Then I nod. "Yeah. I think I am."

I pour myself a mug of coffee and sit across from her. The comforting warmth spreads through my hands into my chest.

Dad strolls into the kitchen, yawning and rubbing the back of his neck. He gives me a hug that smells like aftershave. "Morning, kiddo," he mumbles.

I cling to him a second longer than usual, my eyes stinging. To him, it's just another day. But to me, this moment is everything. Being safe, being home, being held by my dad after a month of wondering if I'd ever see him again.

I will always carry Eric with me, in a part of me that doesn't quite belong to this century anymore. Time didn't stop while I was gone, but somehow, it folded like the pages of a book. Maybe Eric is still somewhere out there, wondering if I made it.

I hope he knows I did. I hope he knows I'll never forget him....

As the sun climbs higher outside the kitchen window, and my family chats about nothing at all, I wrap my hands around my coffee cup, anchor myself to this moment, and let the ache settle quietly beside the joy. I'm home. And that has to be enough.

CHAPTER TWENTY-SEVEN

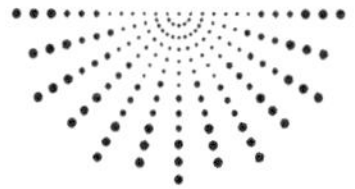

It wasn't even a difficult decision.

By the time the ink dries on the letter, I'm already certain I am following Hattie. My hand doesn't shake as I write it, but my heart thumps in my chest. Not from doubt, but from the ache of everything I'm leaving behind.

Dearest Colin and Levi,

This is not a goodbye you can understand. Just know I love you both. I always have.

I'm chasing something bigger than time, deeper than reason. If I succeed, you may never see me again. But you'll know I lived and that I loved.

Tell Father and Mother I love them. Tell them I carry their strength with me. Everything they taught us, every story by the fire, every hard earned lesson, I won't forget a moment of it. They gave me the roots I needed, and now I'm following my heart where it leads.

Let the others know I'm proud to be their brother. I wish I could've said goodbye in person, but some paths don't leave time for farewells. Tell them to hold tight to each other. To look out for each other.

Brothers, I ask you to grant me this one last request. Never allow my house to be sold. Don't let the land be broken up or my cottage be torn down and built over. Pass down through the generations the importance of keeping our land in the Thomas name. Leave my house in my name. Let it stand. Let the story be told, generation after generation, that one day, I will return.

Until I find my way back,

Eric

I sign it, fold it carefully, and leave it on my desk where I know Colin will find it.

The candle flickers low in its holder, casting golden shadows over the walls I've known all my life. And I'm leaving it behind.

I blow out the candle. Smoke curls in the air like a ghost.

On the porch, the night air wraps around me, cool and damp. The stars are scattered across the sky, and I wonder how different they will look in the future. Will the constellations still be the same? Will Hattie and I sit beneath the same stars, centuries apart?

My boots press into the wet grass as I walk toward my cottage. With every step, I feel lighter and heavier all at once. The pull of the well is real. It's like a rope tied around my ribs, tugging me forward. Toward Hattie. Toward fate. Toward the unknown.

The trees part ahead, revealing the clearing bathed in moonlight. The well gleams softly in the silver light. I spot a figure beside it— hope rising sharply, then falling just as fast. It's not Hattie. It's Charlie.

She's curled on the ground beside the well, her face hidden in her hands, her small shoulders shaking.

"She's gone," Charlie whispers before I can speak.

For a moment, I can't breathe.

Once I steady myself, I reach out and offer her my hand. She takes it, and I help her to her feet. I gently place my hands on her shoulders as we stand facing each other. "Did she say anything before she jumped?" I ask.

Charlie nods without lifting her head. "She said to tell everyone she loved them."

My throat tightens. "She waited?"

"She waited," Charlie says, looking up now. Her face is streaked with tears and dirt. "She kept looking back. But midnight came and went, and she just felt she had to go. You missed her by mere minutes."

I nod, swallowing against the lump in my throat.

"You have to promise me something, Charlie. No matter what happens, no matter how many years go by, you have to protect our land. Make sure my brothers understand. My house, my piece of the Thomas property. It has to stay in the family. Untouched. Preserved."

"For two hundred and fifty years?"

"Yes." My voice cracks. "Because I'm coming back one day, and when I do, I need a place to return to. A place Hattie and I can call home."

"I'll tell them. I swear I will."

"Tell them everything," I plead. "Tell them Hattie and I loved each other enough to risk everything. That it wasn't madness, it was hope. We believed in something stronger than time."

"I will." Charlie crosses her heart with a shaky finger. "I'll tell them every word."

I pull her into a hug, and she clings to me for a moment like a child.

"I wish you didn't have to go, too," she murmurs.

Charlie's just a child, but she's had to carry more loss than most grown people I know. Her brother John died in the battle, bleeding out in the dirt while I held him in my arms. Now Hattie, her closest friend, has stepped into another century, leaving Charlie behind.

I'm next. I see it in her desperate, lonely eyes, red-rimmed with fresh tears. She's losing me, too, and though she nods and says she understands, I know it's another cut on a heart already full of scars.

"I'm sorry, Charlie," I say quietly. "You've lost too much, and now I'm just adding to it."

She shakes her head, but her chin trembles. "I understand. You have to go."

"That doesn't make it right," I whisper. "John… Hattie… now me. It's not fair to you."

Her voice cracks. "I don't want to be the only one left behind."

"I know," I say, my voice thick. "And I wish I could take that pain from you. If I could carry it instead, I would. But I promise, what you're doing matters. Keeping the story alive… it's everything. You're not just being left behind. You're holding the door open for me to come back."

The well stones glow faintly in the moonlight. The air above it hums, charged and alive. I climb up slowly, one leg over, then the other. I glance down. Darkness stares back. And yet, I'm not afraid.

Hattie is on the other side.

I close my eyes for a moment, letting her name steady me. *Hattie.* I see her face. I think of the way she looked at the world, always ready to fight for someone else. I hear her laugh, the one that made everything feel lighter, even in the darkest moments. How she saved my little brother from drowning in the creek. How she had the courage to tell me about the outcome of the battle in an attempt to save my life. She saved the life of an enemy soldier boy and worked around the clock for days, caring for wounded soldiers on both sides. She never turned away from a soul in need. Not once. And now, she's waiting for me.

I remember the way she kissed me before she left. The urgency, trembling, but still soft and sweet.

"Hattie," I whisper into the well. "I'm coming."

And then I jump.

CHAPTER TWENTY-EIGHT

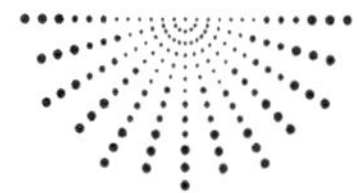

Hattie

After breakfast, I tell my parents and Nina that I'd like to take one last look at the Thomas cottage before we say goodbye to Aunt Ida and head home.

The sun sits high and bright as I walk up the sloping hill toward the edge of the woods. I don't need directions anymore. I know the way by heart.

The trees sway gently overhead, and the rustling leaves sound like whispers. The dry grass crunches beneath my sneakers, and finally, I'm at Eric's cottage.

Time has left its quiet fingerprints all over the little house. Though its bones remain the same, the years have weathered the wood and softened its sharp edges. Ivy clings stubbornly to the stone chimney, as if trying to hold the past in place. Some walls have been rebuilt, newer timber tucked alongside the old, and the windows, once thin panes of hand-blown glass, have been replaced with sturdier, clearer ones.

I climb the steps, floorboards creaking under my feet, and peek in the window. Inside, dust lies thick on every surface, muting the colors and softening the outlines of a life paused.

Stepping back down off the porch, I move around the side, letting my fingertips trail along the hand packed sandstone. The air feels strange. Charged. I pause, looking first at the well and then glancing toward the edge of the woods.

For a moment, I think I see someone standing there. A tall man with dark hair, just like the first time I explored Eric's cottage. A shiver skates down my spine. Who or what can it be? A ghost? A memory?

Maybe that first time I saw Eric, when I thought he was a ghost, it wasn't his ghost at all. Maybe it was a premonition. Something deep inside me recognized what was coming before I could understand. And now, standing here, the memories flood back. The ache. The longing.

I walk closer, my pulse thudding in my ears, and kneel in the tall grass under the big oak, near the place where I was startled and fell in the well.

Where Eric and I made love to each other the first time.

There, nestled in the earth and dappled by the sun, is the stone.

Eric & Hattie.

I blink fast, crouching lower to run my fingers across the worn engraving. The letters are real, solid, cool beneath my touch. Not a dream. Not a fantasy. This stone has been here for centuries. The names carved into the stone are a promise, his and mine, written into time itself.

I stand up, swallowing hard as tears gather, blurring my vision. It was real. It *is* real. I draw in a shaky breath, and as I exhale, the tears finally fall.

"Hattie?"

I whip around. And there he is.

Eric!

He's standing a few yards away, in his work clothes from 1775, looking out of place, but completely perfect.

He runs toward me, and my knees give out. I stumble toward him before I realize I've even moved. Eric catches me. His arms wrap around me, lifting my feet off the ground and spinning me once before settling me into the curve of his chest. His heartbeat thunders under my palm.

And then he lifts my chin and kisses me. Not softly, not hesitantly, but like a man who crossed centuries to find me. The world blurs around us. All I feel is him—warm, solid, and here.

"You're real," I whisper, clutching his biceps. "You're here."

"I told you I'd follow you," he murmurs, his mouth pressed against my hair. "You didn't think I'd let you do all the time traveling, did you?"

I laugh, or maybe sob, I can't tell. "How—when did—how long have you—?"

"I jumped in moments after you did. I was hoping you'd come back to the well soon but was just about to go ask after you at the Monroe house," he says. "I arrived just after you jumped. Charlie was still at the well."

I pull back to look at him fully.

"She was crying," he says softly. "I asked her to make sure the house was preserved. I guess... she really did."

"Of course she did."

Eric smiles, the same crooked smile that melts me. He threads his fingers through mine and glances toward the cottage. "Want to see our house?"

Our house.

I nod, unable to speak. I can't believe he's here.

Inside, the air is heavy with the scent of aged wood and dirt. Sunlight filters through the windows in golden streams, illuminating the dust as it dances lazily through the stillness. Each step we take across the worn floorboards releases a familiar creak, as if the house remembers us.

"I found the deed," Eric says, reaching into his shirt pocket and pulling out a yellowed document folded in thirds. "Exactly where I told them to leave it."

I stare at it, overcome with emotion.

"The Thomas descendants kept the story alive. They remembered. They had everything prepared. Apparently, I've got some pretty devoted family members."

I laugh through my tears. "You left them instructions, and they actually followed them for two hundred and fifty years? I can't even get my students to remember to do their homework."

He shrugs. "I guess I'm persuasive."

We walk through the rooms together, pausing in what used to be the sitting room. He brushes his hand along the old fireplace mantle. I see the glint of emotion in his eyes, and I know, this means everything to him, too. Eric left behind his whole world–his parents, siblings, and dearest friends. All for me.

We return to the Monroe estate, and I squeeze his hand tighter as we walk up the porch steps. Nina is the first to spot us through the window. She bursts through the door, nearly tripping over the threshold, a look of curiosity on her face.

I take a deep breath and say, "Nina, this is Eric."

She looks at him quietly, still trying to process, but offers a small, polite nod. "Hello."

Eric smiles warmly. "Hello, Nina. It's nice to meet you."

I take a steadying breath and step inside with Eric, finding my parents seated in the parlor. Their faces are a mix of intrigue and caution, unsure how to react to the stranger by my side, dressed in clothes from another time.

"Mom, Dad, this is Eric," I say simply, just as I would when introducing a friend. "I met him at the Thomas cottage, the farm just behind the Monroe estate. He's part of the Thomas family."

Eric smiles warmly, stepping forward to greet them. "Mr. and Mrs. Miller, it's a true pleasure to meet you both."

Mom looks him over, carefully, then gently asks, "So you're Aunt Ida's neighbor then? We're glad to meet you, too."

My dad studies Eric's old-fashioned clothing, and I can tell he's about to say something dad-like and embarrassing. "Tell me, Eric... are you Amish, by any chance?"

Eric blinks, surprised, then laughs warmly. "No, sir, not quite. But I do appreciate the sentiment."

The tension eases as my dad chuckles and claps Eric on the shoulder. "Well, you've made a fine first impression either way."

Nina, my parents, Eric, and I spend the day wrapped in the quiet comfort of Aunt Ida's cozy house. As the day begins to pass, I find myself hesitating, the weight of the truth still heavy on my heart. So I persuade them to stay one more day, needing just a little more time to gather the courage, and the right words, to tell my parents that Eric and I have known each other far longer than anyone realizes. I will also eventually have to break it to them that I'll be getting married soon, moving to Massachusetts, and teaching high school here. But that's a conversation for another day.

After dinner, when the sun hangs low and the shadows stretch across the floor, Eric and I follow Aunt Ida into the library.

"We've been expecting you, Mr. Thomas," she says with a knowing smile.

Eric blinks, surprised. "Have you?"

She nods, eyes twinkling. "I told Hattie you'd come home."

I smile and nod. "I wish I had listened better," I admit.

Great Aunt Ida lowers herself into one of the wingback chairs, leans forward slightly, her voice softer. "Charlotte Monroe, or Charlie, as you knew her, played a large role in keeping your story alive. She married your brother Colin. Lived a long, full life. Had children. Told them the story, just as you asked."

Relief washes over me like a gentle tide, upon hearing the news about Charlie and Colin. Knowing that Charlie found happiness and love, marrying Colin after all the hardships they endured, fills a hollow place in my heart I didn't realize was empty. Each of them lost a brother and fought in battle. It's comforting to know they had one another to lean on.

Eric's eyes shine with quiet joy as he reaches for my hand. "Colin always said Charlie was brave and different and that he liked girls with spirit."

"Spirited is an understatement." I lean into him, resting my head on his shoulder.

"Levi and Colin both survived the war," Aunt Ida continues. "Colin passed away in his seventies. Levi made it well into his eighties."

Eric wipes his eyes and nods.

"And Martin, the British soldier boy the Monroe's saved," Ida says, turning to me, "he stayed with the Monroes as a field hand. But eventually he went to Harvard and became one of the best lawyers in Massachusetts. Wrote law books still quoted today."

I cover my mouth with one hand. "Martin!"

As Aunt Ida's words settle over us, Eric and I sit quietly, absorbing all we've learned. She tells Eric about his other siblings and his mother and father, how they spent the rest of their lives.

Aunt Ida gives Eric more details about Charlie, Colin, Levi, Martin, and the way time has held our story gently in its hands. She gives us a knowing smile, as if she's always seen the path that led us here, and then excuses herself to rest.

Hand in hand, Eric and I leave the library, hearts full and quiet, and step out onto the porch. The air is sweet with the scent of honeysuckle, the sky brushed with the pinks, oranges, and lavenders of dusk. We settle onto the old wooden swing. It feels like the Monroe house is finally letting out a breath it's been holding for 250 years.

Eric turns to me "Miss Miller," he says, "what would you say to a summer wedding? Right here at the Monroe estate."

I smile up at him. "I'd say yes."

He kisses my temple. "Good because Great Aunt Ida already gave me her blessing."

I laugh. "She always did know more than she let on."

The breeze picks up, warm and soft against my skin. Fireflies flicker in the distance, and the night feels alive with promise.

I feel Eric's hand in mine. The calluses, the strength, the warmth of a man who crossed centuries for love.

We sit in silence for a while, wrapped in the peace of the moment.

Together and home, at last.

· · ·

THANK YOU FOR READING! BOOK 4, *BACK TO THE HIGHLANDS*, IS NOW available!

ALSO BY ID JOHNSON

Stand Alone Titles

<u>All I Want for Christmas is Pooch</u>

(*sweet contemporary romance*)

<u>Christmas Memory</u>

(*sweet contemporary romance*)

<u>The Doll Maker's Daughter at Christmas</u>

(*clean romance/historical*)

<u>Pretty Little Monster</u>

(*young adult/suspense*)

<u>The Journey to Normal: Our Family's Life with Autism</u> (*nonfiction*)

<u>Found by the Alpha (fantasy romance)</u>

Love Throughout Time

(*time travel romance*)

Back to Titanic

Back to Gettysburg

Back to Bunker Hill

Back to the Highlands

Back to Port Royal

Back to the Spanish Inquisition (coming soon!)

Silverwood Academy

(*paranormal romance*)

Vampire Hunter

World Builder

Realm Jumper

Celestial Springs

(psychological thriller/literary fiction/women's fiction)

Beneath the Inconstant Moon

The First Mrs. Edwards

Leaving Ginny

The Motherhood

(dystopian romance)

Rain's Rebellion

Rain's Run

Rain's Return

Ashes and Rose Petals

(contemporary romance/retelling of Romeo and Juliet and Cinderella)

Girl in the Attic

Girl From the Tomb

Girl On the Beach

Nashville Country Dreams

(contemporary romance)

Meant to Marry Me

Lead Me Home

You Are the Reason

Forever Love series

(clean romance/historical)

Cordia's Will: A Civil War Story of Love and Loss

Cordia's Hope: A Story of Love on the Frontier

The Clandestine Saga series

(paranormal romance)

Transformation

Resurrection

Repercussion

Absolution

Illumination

Destruction

Annihilation

Obliteration

Termination

A Vampire Hunter's Tale (based on The Clandestine Saga)

(paranormal/alternate history)

Aaron

Jamie

Elliott

Christian

The Chronicles of Cassidy (based on The Clandestine Saga)

(young adult paranormal)

So You Think Your Sister's a Vampire Hunter?

Who Wants to Be a Vampire Hunter?

How Not to Be a Vampire Hunter

My Life As a Teenage Vampire Hunter

Vampire Hunting Isn't for Morons

Vampires Bite and Other Life Lessons

Gone Guardian

Death Does Not Become Her

Blood of the Vampire Hunter (based on The Clandestine Saga)

(paranormal romance)

Night Slayer

Shadow Stalker

Queen Catcher

Mother Hunter

Father Finder

Ghosts of Southampton series

(historical romance)

Prelude

Titanic

Residuum

Lusitania

Heartwarming Holidays Sweet Romance series

(Christian/clean romance)

Melody's Christmas

Christmas Cocoa

Winter Woods

Waiting On Love

Shamrock Hearts

A Blossoming Spring Romance

Firecracker!

Falling in Love

Thankful for You

Melody's Christmas Wedding

The New Year's Date

Charles Town Brides (based on Heartwarming Holidays Sweet Romance)

(Christian/clean romance)

From This Moment

Can't Help Falling in Love

It's Your Love

When You Say Nothing At All

My Girl

Unchained Melody

I Only Have Eyes For You

At Last

The Very Thought of You

Reaper's Hollow

(paranormal/urban fantasy)

Ruin's Lot

Ruin's Promise

Ruin's Legacy

When Kings Collide

(steamy historical romance)

Princess of Silence

Princess of Hearts

Collections

Ghosts of Southampton Books 0-2

Reaper's Hollow Books 1-3

The Clandestine Saga Books 1-3

The Chronicles of Cassidy Books 1-4

Celestial Springs Collection

Heartwarming Holidays Sweet Romance Books 1-3

Heartwarming Holidays Sweet Romance Books 4-7

Websites: https://books2read.com/ap/xX7ZD8/ID-Johnson

For updates, visit www.authoridjohnson.blogspot.com

Follow on Twitter @authoridjohnson

Find me on Facebook at www.facebook.com/IDJohnsonAuthor

Instagram: @authoridjohnson

Follow me on Bookbub: https://www.bookbub.com/authors/id-johnson